RUNT OF THE PACK

SILVANA G. SÁNCHEZ

BOOKS BY SILVANA G. SÁNCHEZ

CURSED KINGDOMS

Ash and Snow

Steel and Stone

VESELY ACADEMY

Academy of Extraordinary Creatures

The Soul Thief

Curse the Moon

The Blood of Kings

THE UNNATURAL BRETHREN

Written in Blood

Call of Blood

Cast in Blood

Midnight Kiss

BAD BOY SHIFTERS OF THE

UNNATURAL BRETHREN

Branded in Love

Runt of the Pack

Embers of Fate

*Be the first to know when Silvana's next book is available!
Follow her on Bookbub to get an alert whenever she has a
new release, preorder, or discount!*

*For the wolves among us,
and the power of the pack.*

*And for you, wonderful reader.
(Don't hate me.
You'll thank me later.)*

It's not of love that I die, I die of you.
I die of you, love, of love of you.
Of an urgent need of mine, of my skin,
  for you;
of my soul for you, and of my mouth.
And of the unbearable man that I am
  without you.

— JAIME SABINES

A NOTE FROM THE AUTHOR

The events that take place in this story occurred four years after the ones related in *Branded in Love*, a year before those narrated in *Cast in Blood*.

As you navigate through Vladimir and Anya's story, you will see how intricately it is intertwined with Gavriil's descent into darkness—essentially, how he became a '*villain*'.

As always, I ask you to refrain from judging any of these cherished characters. In this world, much like the one we live in, you will find there are no clear-cut heroes and villains. Instead, there are merely individuals (albeit *exceptional* ones) trying their best with the limited resources available to them amid challenging situations.

If you are new to these characters, I hope you will

delight in witnessing the love story of Vlad and Anya. And if this glimpse into their world intrigues you, I recommend reading the Unnatural Brethren series afterwards.

Until then...
In love and gratitude,
Silvana.

RUNT OF THE PACK

When the lone wolf claims his fated mate, the pack bounds will be tested.

The runt of the pack. An Alpha redeemed.
Vladimir Volkov, leader of the Roman wolf pack, seeks vengeance when an old enemy returns to Russia. But tragedy strikes, and Vlad fails his duty to the Ursa clan. Left for dead after a brutal fight, a white wolf revives him. Given new life, he vows to prove himself to his pack again. But there's one thing he never expected to find along the way—his fated mate.

Spurned by the pack. An Omega's rising.

Rogue omega Anya Sokolov lives alone, painting to survive. Her wolf craves more. A howl in a snowstorm leads her to a wounded stranger—her fated mate, Vladimir. But joy turns to chaos when Anya's pack Alpha finds her. Old wounds reopen, threatening her newfound happiness with Vladimir.

RUNT OF THE PACK

VLADIMIR VOLKOV

I creep down the stone hallway, my feet silent on the cold floor. I'm supposed to be in lessons, but I had to see Father. Tomorrow is my sixteenth birthday, and I want to ask him about my family. My real family.

Most shifter pups come into their power and transform for the first time at sixteen. I want answers before I shift.

Voices drift from Father's study—his deep baritone and the raspy tones of his advisers. I sneak up to the heavy wooden door left slightly ajar and peer through the crack. Father sits at his desk, brow furrowed as he speaks.

"...the boy is coming along well in his studies, but he'll never have the raw strength of my Gavriil."

"Very kind of you to take in the runt, my king," an adviser says. "Not every pack is so generous with the weak ones."

My heart drops into my stomach. Me? I'm... weak?

Father sighs. "His birth pack did right leaving him. The mountains are no place for a runt. But it wasn't the boy's fault how he was born."

"Of course, my King. Your benevolence lives up to Your Majesty's greatness."

Tears burn in my eyes. Father only took me in because he pitied me? Because I was small and weak? Is that why my real family didn't want me?

I back away from the door, my young heart shattered. I was abandoned... because I'm a runt.

I will never be good enough.

PRESENT DAY

1

VLAD

Rome, Italy.

*R*ain pours down as I unleash a barrage of strikes against the training dummy. My fists pound the padded leather, each hit thunderous and unchecked. I weave and lunge with predatory speed, visualizing enemies surrounding me.

My pack gathers under the shelter of stone, watching as I train shirtless in the downpour. Rivulets trace the ridges of my powerful frame, soaking into the fur of the twin wolves inked across my right arm.

With a final crushing kick, the dummy's head

rockets through the air. My audience roars as I turn to them, chest heaving.

"Let's see if the rest of you can match your Alpha," I call out, tossing Pietro a staff. The pack laughs and steps into the rain to spar.

I pluck the dummy head from the mud and squeeze until it splits into two pieces, falling to the ground. No one thought I was meant to lead. But I have forged myself into the warrior I am today. An Alpha who bows to no one.

My tactical boots echo on the cold marble steps as I stride back into the sprawling estate, rain dripping from my body, adrenaline still coursing through my veins. A hot shower washes away the chill rain, but unease lingers in my gut.

Once dressed in a bespoke Oxford grey suit, four stone-faced betas flank me as I descend to the first floor. We move down the manor's cavernous halls lit by iron sconces, and I detect subtle notes of anxiety tainting the air. My inner wolf bristles.

Luca, a slender beta with sharp features, approaches me in the grand foyer framed by towering marble columns. "Alpha Vlad, Enrico awaits you in the parlor," he says, eyes downcast submissively.

I nod and move forward without a word. The parlor's intricate double doors groan as betas Luca and Paulo open them in unison. Inside, Enrico stands swiftly, tension in his hunched shoulders.

"What news?" I demand, steeling myself, although my heart quickens now that I stand seconds away from hearing the answer.

But before Enrico can respond, the parlor doors burst open again. Two more betas drag a battered and bloodied wolf shifter into the room. He whimpers and struggles against their grip.

I recognize him instantly—Antonio, one of my newest recruits. Fresh from Naples. My eyes narrow as I take in his wounds, his shredded clothing. "What is the meaning of this?"

"Apologies, Alpha," Paulo says. "We discovered this omega fleeing from a territorial battle. He deserted his own to save himself."

Antonio won't meet my gaze.

A heavy silence settles in the room. To abandon one's packmates, even in the face of defeat—it's the greatest dishonor for our kind. Inside me, two wolves war. The Alpha, incensed by such cowardice. The omega runt, who once believed himself too weak to lead or fight.

"There can be no forgiveness for such betrayal," Luca spits. Murmurs of agreement echo from the others.

Slowly, I approach Antonio, now trembling before me. Still a youth, barely twenty. Eyes full of fear and shame. He does not see a powerful leader standing over him now—only the ruthless pack that abandoned their unwanted omega so long ago.

My voice is steel when I speak, though my heart wars with pity. "You renounced your vows to your pack. Therefore, you shall be renounced by this one. No clan can harbor a deserter."

I grip Antonio's chin hard, forcing his eyes to meet my own. "But loyalty and sacrifice can repay even the deepest dishonor. Prove this to me... and perhaps you may find your place in my pack again."

I release him with a shove. "Take him. He's banned from these lands until his redemption." Stunned silence follows as Antonio is dragged away. An omega granted a second chance—unheard of in our ancient traditions. But mercy and trust shall bind my pack... not fear.

I turn back to Enrico, who waits patiently despite the sudden interruption. My heartbeat spikes, reminded of why my Enforcer requested this meeting. Whatever news he's uncovered must be important enough to risk my wrath at the disruption.

"You were saying?" I prompt. I clasp my hands behind my back to hide their shaking.

Enrico lifts his chin. "Yes, Alpha. My news." He pauses, as if gathering courage. "*We've found him*, my Alpha," he begins.

Instantly, I stiffen, my hands curled into tight fists out of their own accord. I've been waiting for this moment for almost a decade. Grisha—the vicious snake who betrayed my brother Gavriil and murdered Bella, his first mate. I swore a blood oath to my brother to deliver Grisha's wretched head on a spike. At last, we have him. *Almost.*

"Where?" I am curt.

"Grisha Vorobyev was spotted in Sestroretsk." Enrico meets my glare. "Near your brother's summer home."

"Fuck!" I growl. "Gavriil is there on holiday... with his human mate, Luciana." When my gaze cuts to my Enforcer's, he understands. If Grisha dared show his face in Sestroretsk, it can only mean one thing—he plots against Gavriil once more.

"Ready my jet," I command the betas, my voice deathly quiet. They bow and swiftly depart. "Enrico, you remain in charge during my absence," I tell my enforcer.

He bows low. "Of course, Alpha. I will not fail you. However..." his words drift into silence.

I frown. "Well?" I utter impatiently. "Speak."

He swallows hard. "I don't think you should go alone, my Alpha," he finally says. "At least allow me to set up a team. They could—"

"That is out of the question," I dismiss.

"But, Alpha Vladimir..."

"This is something I must do on my own," I say, my tone leaving no room for discussion.

I stride out of the room, visions of Grisha's dying screams already flashing through my mind. He will pay in blood and fear for betraying my family and harming my brother. And his death by my hand will prove to Gavriil that despite the rift between us, blood runs thicker than water.

As I prepare for departure, rage and icy purpose fill me.

"I'm coming for you, Grisha," I vow under my breath.

2

ANYA

Sestroretsk, Russia.

The biting wind whips through my threadbare coat as I move across the long driveway, canvas clutched tightly in my grasp. Ahead, Yulia Lebedev's imposing doors loom like a beacon, promising shelter from the icy gusts.

It's been five months, and I still can't believe my luck, that the eccentric former art curator would stumble upon one of my paintings in a quaint shop in town. Luckier still, that she has steadily commissioned me for her grand hotel projects ever since.

Thanks to her, my wintry landscapes now grace the walls of prestigious hotels like the Ritz and Hyatt in Moscow. Deep down, I can't help but feel a twinge of disappointment at how my art is simply reduced to mere decor. However, with the harsh winter months upon us, securing food and warmth remains my sole priority.

I press the ornate doorbell, its melodic chime echoing inside the manor. Rubbing my numb fingers, I wait for the housekeeper to answer.

The massive door soon swings open, revealing Yulia Lebedev herself rather than a servant. She's a woman in her mid-sixties, tall and rail-thin, with an elaborate bouffant of platinum blonde hair. Her shrewd grey eyes fix on me as she waves a beringed hand.

"Anya! Come in, come in!" she says. "Let's get you out of this dreadful chill."

Yulia ushers me inside, her long ostrich feather coat swirling dramatically around her as she closes out the winter air. Bold styles suit her imperious temperament.

"Good day, Yulia," I greet her dutifully. With great care, I unwrap the layers of brown paper protecting my latest piece, a moonlit snowscape rendered in icy silvers and blues.

Yulia's keen eyes widen as she takes in the painting. "Magnificent as always, my dear! Now come, let's get you warmed up with some tea..."

She links her arm through mine and steers us further into the manor's warmth, nattering on about her grand plans for my work. I simply nod along, allowing her to claim the conversation as I soak up the respite from the elements.

We lounge in an opulent parlor, and soon, the bitter cold outside seems a distant dream. Yulia's eyes widen as she takes in the painting. "The colors are so vibrant, even with your limited winter palette. Such light captured on the snow beneath that majestic pine..."

She looks up at me, smiling. "However do you stand out there in the cold long enough to envision such scenes, my girl?" Shaking her head in wonder, she motions for me to follow further inside, out of the bitter wind still gusting through the open door. "Oh, but I know better than to steal an artist's secrets." She offers me a warm, teasing expression.

Setting down the small porcelain cup, I force a smile, clamping down on my aggrieved wolf within, howling at the loss of yet another painting. But Yulia is right. I do have a secret, and carefully keep it hidden. My wolf is the sole reason vivid nature scenes like this one flow from my brush, rather than what dull human memory alone could provide.

In the midnight hours, I prowl across isolated forest paths on four steady paws rather than two legs, white fur shielding the tender skin from winter's worst. With a wolf's sharp sight, I commit to perfect memory snow-laden boughs gleaming radiant under the full moon's glow.

My inner wolf sets free during these secret runs. The time spent with her gives me the strength to stand tall and face those who would look down on a solitary outcast like myself.

I trail behind Yulia as she sweeps into a grandiose office at the end of the hall. Her features turn somber as she halts behind the impressive desk. "Have you heard about the storm coming?" she asks, her hand gently resting on the golden handle of a drawer.

I shake my head.

"It's going to hit tonight, after midnight. They're saying it could be the worst one in years." Her voice drops to a cautious whisper. "I know your dacha is rather secluded. Will you be safe, my dear?"

"I'll manage," I say tightly. My wolf bristles, indignant at the perceived pity. I am no longer an omega. It's been almost a year since I was cast out from the Alpha Krov pack. I can take care of myself now.

Yulia pulls an envelope from the drawer and joins me in the center of the room. Her brow creases with concern as she presses it into my hand. I thank her and tuck it into my coat pocket before heading for the door.

She escorts me to the vestibule. "I'll see you in three weeks, then," Yulia says, "with the next couple of paintings?"

"Sure." I nod, my footsteps echoing on the marble floor.

As the doors open, a blast of frigid air hits me, stealing away what little warmth I had gathered.

We exchange farewells and I head back to my place, the weak sun mocking me as it dips below the trees. There are still hours left before the impending storm, but my wolf urges me to hurry. She remembers our first days of exile—the cruel winter storms that ravaged us, the constant struggle for food...

My legs pump furiously as I sprint through the dense woods, snowflakes beginning to blanket the ground. Soon, the rundown cabin appears, a welcome refuge. With no time to waste, I chop wood with vigor, stockpile it by the door. The ax handle stings my palms, but I welcome the pain. It's honest work, the work of survival.

Inside, I strip the dacha of all but the essentials, stowing boxes in the cellar. The wind howls fiercely outside as the sun begins to set, sending icy daggers through the walls. But we are ready, my wolf and I. Come what may, we will endure together.

I pause as the fire sputters to life, warding off the creeping twilight. But while the iron stove promises warmth, it cannot soothe my wolf—now pacing impatiently within our confined refuge. My inner beast recalls the freedom of running wild beneath the moonlight unencumbered. Tonight though, only the shrieking storm awaits beyond barred doors.

"Not tonight, girl..." I grumble as I gather my painting oils, tossing them into their small crate. A sigh escapes me as I glance over the unfinished canvas. My hands itch to create, but my mind is too consumed with worry and frustration to find any inspiration.

Meanwhile, my wolf stirs restlessly, longing to answer winter's violent song with our own ululating cry. She urges me to venture out one last time, free from the confines of walls and ceilings.

When she reminds me that this could be our final

glimpse of the shimmering lake before it freezes over, I am trapped in her wild excitement.

3

VLAD

Rain continues to pelt the tarmac of Ciampino Airport as I stride towards my sleek private Gulfstream jet. The icy night air slides over my skin, barely registered. My heart pounds with focused intent—reach my brother and remove the threat slithering in his territory before it strikes.

My boots echo loudly on the empty boarding steps. Inside, the luxurious jet cabin provides no comfort, its plush ivory leather chairs and polished wood surfaces barely glimpsed. With sharp gestures, I direct my pilot Andre to file our urgent flight plan to Pulkovo as the last suitcases are loaded. We must be wheels up within thirty minutes if we're to reach Russia tonight.

Settling into my seat facing the length of the

plane, I tap the armrest impatiently. Useless to pace the confines of the jet, yet remaining still proves impossible. My knee bounces rapidly as the engines rumble to life, power flooding my tense muscles. I crave action, but can only endure this helpless waiting as we taxi onto the runway.

As the jet lifts smoothly into the dark sky, the city lights of Rome dropping rapidly behind us, the weight of dread settles heavier in my gut. When I carve Grisha's heart from his worthless chest with my claws, I'll be certain Gavriil learns to be wary of the company he keeps.

Unable to tolerate further inaction, I retrieve my phone to warn my brother of the viper I now race to intercept. No doubt in his arrogant ways, Gavriil believes himself untouchable even as peril encroaches. *блядь!* One ring echoes after another with no answer —the pup's probably knot-deep in his pretty human pet instead of taking my call. Never mind she warms his bed, no ordinary mortal can understand our ancient bonds and ways.

Frustrated, I slam the phone down, cracking the screen. A fierce growl rumbles in my chest. If Gavriil is too distracted by his plaything to address this threat, perhaps his Enforcer isn't likewise compromised. I jab Sasha's number next. He at least carries centuries of duty to our clan in his blood and bones.

Three rings before voicemail picks up. My fangs punch free as a red haze clouds my vision for a brief, savage moment. I force a breath, wrestling the wolf back under control. We'll have the traitor's blood soon enough. When Sasha also fails to answer after several more attempts, unease replaces my rage. Why does no one respond? Has the attack already begun while I waste precious hours trapped uselessly in flight?

A shrill beep pierces my spiraling thoughts—the secure satellite line reserved for high-level pack emergencies. Impossible to ignore. I slam my hand on the receiver.

"What?" My demand echoes through the silent cabin. Surely, it's not Gavriil on the line. He never calls himself, even when his tail bleeds, always working through retainers.

Static hisses across the connection. Frustrated, I repeat the sharp query, prepared to ream whichever incompetent underling interrupts me. A hesitant female voice finally answers, so quiet the words are nearly lost under the white noise crackle.

"Volodya? I'm sorry, I know I should not be calling you like this..."

"Samara?" I blurt in surprise. I haven't heard my sister's voice in years, not since she rejected the bear I suggested as her mate. Her timid presence used to quietly smooth many childhood fights and tensions back when Gavriil and I constantly circled each other as competitive pups.

Concern strikes bone-deep as I register her breathless tone. Sam never initiates conversations, much less emergency contact. She murmurs confirmation of her identity, almost drowned out by increasingly loud static. I activate the sat phone controls to adjust signal clarity. "What's happened? Why are you calling?"

"...attacked... estate compromised..." is all I can pick out.

"Sammy, speak up!" I grip the phone tightly in rising apprehension. "Has the estate been attacked? Is Gavriil in danger?"

"Can't... long... not safe..." More static, the white noise now completely overriding her voice. Damning useless technology! I should rely instead on true wolf hearing.

In one smooth motion, I unfasten my seatbelt and drop to the plush carpet on all fours. The primal stance focuses my senses, nerves thrumming with effort to receive Sam's faint voice through the miles between us. Heartbeats slip past as I filter out the jet noise and push my hearing to its heightened limits. Like plunging into dark water, I strain everything searching for that one dim lifeline.

Bands of steel slowly encase my chest as each breath struggles harder against its crushing pressure. Echoes of chaos suddenly scream from the phone abandoned by my knee—shouts of pain and fury, gun blasts, and roaring flames. The sharp reek of silver cuts through the smoke. Then, louder than all the carnage—a resonant fatal roar of agony. Shock whites my vision for long seconds.

My brother's roar.

No!

A ferocious snarl rips from my throat. That death keen heralds the most devastating loss imaginable—an Alpha robbed of their destined mate. The severed bond's ruthless agony has driven weaker shifters instantly insane. What could have happened to so horribly wound my strong sibling?

I return to a human posture, hand shaking violently as I raise the receiver once more. But only a cold dial tone answers now, the brief unstable call terminated. Bloody hell, this barely controlled panic must stop! I brace my hands hard against the floor, harnessing sheer willpower to cage the terror-fueled wolf fighting my mental barriers. My quivering muscles labor against the restraint with lethal intent, recognizing the threat hunting our kin.

None stand with us when we defend our own! I must reach his side immediately and tear the responsible traitors apart myself!

With stubborn resolve, I force the wolf back once more. Savage vengeance cannot manifest untethered at 30,000 feet, no matter how fiercely it claws for release. I need answers, not reactions... and if catastrophe truly has come, I will need a clear mind to salvage anything from the aftermath.

Shakily, I resume my seat, eyeing the silent phone with renewed dread. Its brief fragmented message carried no details about what ripped such agony from my brother, whether Luciana and my sister still draw breath... I cannot lose them. Not when family bonds lay so dangerously frayed already. Forthcoming tears burn in my eyes. Maybe Gavriil yet survives, despite that terrible omen—please, let him endure long enough for me to save them all!

I inhale a steadying breath as Father's voice echoes through my mind. *"Family and duty come first, my son. Without them, no shifter can claim honor."* I failed my duties before, leaving Gavriil to pick up the pieces of our legacy alone when Father died. But I will not fail him again. If any chance remains to preserve what family I have left, I must seize it with both hands.

The jet shudders slightly in a patch of turbulence. I glance at the windows, but the night sky reveals no answers. Grim experience warns me such unsteady currents often portend a gathering storm. Raking my fingers roughly through my hair, I reach for my customary emotional control, forced to acknowledge circumstances now spiral far beyond my influence.

I detest disorder or variables muddling careful strategy. But chaos fuels Grisha's insatiable ambition... how perfectly it serves his depraved purpose that I race blindly into the maelstrom left in his wake. Clenching my fists until my knuckles crack, I silently swear crushing vengeance against the mutt and any allied with him. For too long have our enemies hounded us without proper retaliation. *No more.* Any who dare bring harm to my family will drown in rivers of blood.

A hesitant touch grazes my arm. "Alpha?" Andre stands before me, concern and confusion darkening his brown eyes. My volatile reaction startles him. "We caught a bad altitude bounce. Please let me know if you need anything."

No doubt he assumes the turbulence triggered my agitation. I inhale slowly, smoothing impatience from my tone before responding. "Give me an update on our flight plan. Have we crossed the Alps yet?"

"Yes, Alpha. We're halfway over Austria right now."

I nod. "Very good. Carry on then."

As Andre withdraws gratefully to the cockpit, I steady my nerves once more. We are less than two hours from Russia now. Surely, my brother holds enough power and skill to sustain his defense that long. But if Grisha leverages black magic or demonic allies against him, even an Ursa King could fall without warning. Dammit! I should demand this aircraft fly faster.

I must keep faith in Gavriil's smug confidence, if nothing else. He always bragged our family's guardian star shone brighter than for any other shifter clan. I ignored his boasting as puerile myth when we were young, secure in Father's might and status. Now, with an enemy's venom spreading ruin through the heart of our lineage, what choice remains but to trust in luck... or destiny? Surely, the fates would never permit a mere cur like Grisha to sever the proud Alexeev heritage stretching back for millennia.

But fate did decree I rise to an Alpha when all branded me as a doomed omega. She also set brother against brother until the bonds of blood were no longer bound. I now defend the very pack I was once accused of betraying just because I fought to claim my own, rather than lick Gavriil's fur and fill his mead cup… If he expects me to crawl whimpering back to the Ursa after this crisis, I will send his pelt as my reply. The pup threw me aside first—it shames my dignity to stand cold and begging at his door like some kicked stray.

Although… perhaps when he sees how fortune clearly favors me in the coming battle, he will welcome this black wolf home again. The pack always circles closest around the fangs that protect them. I must be the warrior the Ursa requires once more.

I quell my seething frustration to lift my gaze towards the shadowed heaven beyond the window glass. The stars dazzle brilliantly tonight, sharp enough to pierce even a wolf's razor sight. One gleams slightly brighter than the rest—our shepherd Alpha Lupi, ever guarding his wayward children below. Standing witness as we rend each other again in the old vicious cycle. But no more… this time, a new moon rises for House Volkov.

Tonight, I will save them all and demand the honor rightfully owed. Gavriil can offer no further protest once my power restores what his weakness surrendered. The Ursa will joyfully acknowledge a fierce Alpha prepared to bleed in their defense. And my lost brother will finally welcome me home with pride. Fate promised me redemption... I have only to seize it.

We race towards destiny now, one foretold eons past yet somehow still mine to shape. I readily embrace the challenge, unafraid of any reckoning to come. The runt survives when the Alpha cannot, after all. When the battle rages and even Gavriil lies broken, I will prevail against the darkness.

Upon my life, I so vow.

4

VLAD

The tires of my white Audi scrape and slip over patches of black ice as I race up the serpentine mountain road towards the Alexeev dacha. The sprawling summer mansion is perched high on the hill, standing sentinel over our clan's ancestral territory. Gavriil was meant to be safe here. If any harm has befallen him, retribution will be swift.

The iron gates of the dacha finally loom out of the darkness ahead, flanked by twin stone bears on the snow-laden path. I brake hard and throw the car into park, not even bothering to pull into the garage. The front door hangs open, a flickering light visible within. My hackles rise as I approach, my wolf senses detecting the lingering scent of violence in the air. I step inside and see the foyer in shambles—antique vases shattered, mahogany furniture overturned and splintered. My hands clench into fists.

"Gavriil!" I bellow. My voice echoes through the cavernous rooms but there is no answer save for the howling wind outside. I follow the destruction into the main hall, unease coiling tighter with each step. Smears of blood mar the once pristine marble floors. Its metallic tang violently fills my nostrils. A growl rumbles in my chest. Whose blood is it? My brother's... or his enemies'?

The blown-open French doors at the end of the hall show snow swirling beyond onto the deck. Boot prints track crimson stains across the threshold into the night. So, the confrontation began inside before spilling into the open wilderness. Gavriil is out there, somewhere. Wounded, or hunting. And he's not alone.

I stalk back down the hallway, fury and dread coursing through my veins with each pounding heartbeat. In the foyer, I spot Dimitri's body, his throat savagely slashed. But I do not mourn the loss of this member of the Ursa Elite—the fool brought this fate upon himself by failing to safeguard my kin. Now Gavriil's life hangs in the balance.

I continue my determined stalk, the delicious taste of retribution flooding my senses and drowning out the coppery stench of blood that pervades the atmosphere. My footfalls echo ominously off the vaulted ceilings and marble floors now scarred by violence.

Soon, more bodies come into view. Four in total —interloping strangers marked with the crest of Grisha's clan. My lip curls at the sight of them.

The first lies sprawled at the bottom of the carved staircase, spine twisted unnaturally, his open dead eyes staring into oblivion. Another is slumped halfway through an arched doorway, the carved wood stained a glistening red where his head lolls back, mouth open in a silent scream. His throat is no longer fully attached.

Farther down the hall, a trail of gore leads to two more fallen assassins. One, only a boy scarcely old enough to stand with the pack, is crumpled on his side like a discarded doll, the gaping tear in his throat still leaking precious lifeblood across the intricately tiled floor. His companion lies collapsed across him, as if vainly trying to shield the youth from their shared gruesome fate.

At the end of the corridor awaits the grand foyer where Dimitri lies. I step disdainfully over the corpses of my faceless enemies, their rogue pack crest the only detail of interest about them now.

Just then, my sharpened wolf's senses pick up two familiar scents—Gavriil's essence, and Luciana's lilac perfume. But my sister Samara's scent is absent, bringing me some small relief. Wherever she is, it seems she avoided this bloodbath.

Shucking off my long leather coat, I shift into my wolf form with a guttural snarl. Sleek obsidian fur ripples over powerful muscles as my claws and fangs elongate. The scents in the house intensify tenfold through my lupine senses—blood, fear, rage. And overlaying it all, a sickening trace I know well. The stench of one who has turned traitor. *Grisha.*

Jaws snapping, I bound out the broken doors into the snow-blanketed woods. The freezing wind lashes my face but I welcome the pain, letting it sharpen my focus. I open my maw, drawing in deep gulps of air to catch my brother's scent. There—the faintest essence of pine and woodsmoke, uniquely his, off to the northeast. I spring after it in pursuit, paws flying swiftly over the frozen ground.

I have tracked many enemies through these woods over long, bloody years. Every twisting trail and moon-silvered glade is familiar to me even in darkness. My brother's scent leads me deep into the pines, to a narrow ravine spanned by an ancient fallen tree. I creep low, ears pricked. The gurgle of the half-frozen stream masks any sounds of movement. Has he come this way or his hunters?

A scream suddenly shatters the stillness—high, sharp, female. I bolt towards it, ice crashing through the underbrush until I come upon a small, snow-covered clearing. There I find a massive brown bear lumbering towards a trembling figure—a young blonde woman, crouching against a tree, clutching her bloodied arm.

Luciana. Her wide eyes widen further at the sight of my wolf.

With a savage snarl, I launch myself onto the bear's back. We crash down in a violent tangle of fangs and claws. I end the threat swiftly, my jaws tearing into the vulnerable throat until the beast lies still.

"Vladimir?!" she gasps out, body sagging in relief.

In a heartbeat, I shift back to human form, kneeling by her side. "What happened? Where are the others?" I demand. She flinches as I examine the gashes torn across her forearm—claw marks, but from no ordinary beast.

"They came for us!" her lips tremble as she whispers, tears slipping down her snow-flecked cheeks. "Bear shifters!"

Rage flares hotly in my gut at her words. Grisha's

rogue clan nearly killed Gavriil years ago. And now, they've resurfaced to threaten us again. Treacherous scum.

"Gavriil… he's hurt. He went after Grisha. He's the only one left. Oh, Gavriil! I don't know if he's still alive!" Despair sweeps over her as she shudders in dismay.

"Where is he?" I demand, rage igniting like an inferno inside me. But shaken in shock, she can't seem to hear me. "Luciana, listen to me… Listen!" I grasp her face firmly in my hands, forcing her to meet my gaze. "Where—is—Grisha?"

At the sound of his name, fury burns away her fear. "He did this to me before Gavriil took him away." Luciana points a shaking hand towards the trees on the far side of the clearing.

My blood pounds like thunder in my ears. Grisha was my most trusted sentry until he betrayed us. He murdered Bella, his rabid bear too furious to recognize his own lover. It nearly cost Gavriil's life.

"Come on. We've gotta move." I help Luciana to her feet, ready to resume the hunt. But as I turn towards the trees, a resounding crack echoes from their depths—the heavy tread of a large beast stalking closer.

At once, I push Luciana behind me and shift

before she can cry out. Bones grind and pop, muscles surge and swell. My claws sink deep into the frozen earth as I place myself between her and our hunter.

A monstrous shape lurches from the pines, fur as black as pitch. The grizzly's frame ripples with unnatural size and strength—no normal animal, but a formidable shifter. *Grisha.* His beady eyes fix on me and his lips peel back to reveal curved yellow fangs.

A rumbling hiss seethes from his throat in a single word: "Vlad."

My answering roar shakes the night. Traitor and betrayer, hunter and prey—know each other well. He has stolen innocence and spilled clan blood tonight. There will be no mercy for him now.

With stunning speed, the bear charges straight for us. I rush to meet him head-on, our forms colliding like boulders in the ravine. We slam to the frozen ground, all claws and snapping jaws. A swipe of his massive paw knocks me aside and then we are circling, snarling, waiting for an opening.

When Grisha lunges again, I twist lithely away, going for his exposed flank. My fangs find purchase, but only briefly as his thick hide turns my bite. He whirls with a bellow, striking me hard across the muzzle. I roll with the force of it then spring up and dive beneath him, tearing at the tender skin of his underbelly. Hot blood splatters on the snow.

The grizzly rears up with a deafening roar. I brace for his next attack... but instead, he whirls and crashes into the trees, back towards the clearing's edge. Towards Luciana.

No, no, no!

She stands frozen in horror, unable to flee the towering beast charging right at her.

"NOOOOO!" The cry tears from my throat in a desperate howl as I lunge after Grisha, but I am too late. Luciana's scream ends in a sickening crunch beneath his swiping claws. Her broken body flies from view over the cliff's edge. Agony and fury roar through me. The fire of vengeance burns through my blood—her death shall not go unpunished.

With a savage roar, I throw myself at Grisha's exposed flank, clamping my jaws tight around his thick neck until I taste blood. He bellows and thrashes but I hold fast, shaking my head violently as we slam against the trees. I will tear out his vile throat if it's the last thing I do on this earth.

A piercing shriek rumbles from his throat as Grisha rears up and then crashes down, his full weight crushing me to the frozen ground. My grip breaks as he thrashes free. I try to rise, but my left foreleg buckles beneath me, broken. Before I can brace myself, Grisha's head swings around, massive jaws clamping over my shoulder and back, fangs sinking deep into muscle and sinew. He shakes me violently like prey until my vision spins sickeningly. Then with one final roar, he hurls me away from him. I slam brutally against the trunk of an ancient pine before slumping broken to its roots.

Through the haze of agony, I watch the grizzly turn and flee into the woods, following some unseen trail. *Gavriil.* He's still hunting my brother, leaving me to die.

He's alive... Gavriil is still alive...

I try to drag myself upright, to shift forms and give chase, but my ruined body will no longer obey. My wolf's limbs lie useless beneath me as my lifeblood stains the innocent snow. All I can do is raise my muzzle skyward and let loose a mournful howl that echoes endlessly through the icy woods.

I have shamed my kin, my bloodline, and the very essence of who I am... a disgrace to my pack.

5

ANYA

The full moon hangs heavy and bright in the jet sky as I step outside into the icy night. I pause on the dacha's creaking porch, eyes falling shut as I tilt my head back, inhaling the crisp winter air. My breath mists before me in swirling white plumes.

Shedding my coat, I welcome the bite of the frigid wind on my bare skin. I welcome the cold, the freedom it brings. With lithe steps, I descend into the snow-laden yard, leaving behind the confines of walls and ceilings. Out here, I am bound by nothing.

My spine ripples as I lower to all fours. Muscles shift, bones crack and reform. In moments, white fur sprouts over tender flesh and I emerge reborn—a she-wolf with moon-bright eyes.

At last, I spring forward, paws gliding swiftly and surely over the frosted land. The powdery snow muffles the drum of my footfalls. I weave between the ink-black trunks of the sleeping forest, unhindered by branches that bar a human's way. The cold night enfolds me in its loving embrace.

I reach the cliffs overlooking the frozen lake. The wind's violent hands cannot touch me here. I prowl along the precipice, wolf and woman both drinking in the sight of moon-kissed ice locked still and silent below. This winter ocean, both beautiful and bleak, fills us with joy and sorrow mingled. Come spring, its shimmering surface will flow free once more. But tonight it gleams, a reminder that all things have their season.

Somewhere in the distance, a lone wolf howls a haunting song to the moon's opal face. Its cry is laced with a sorrow that pierces my heart. I understand its message all too well—*agony*. I lift my head to the sky once more, joining my voice to the lonely wolf's cry.

My she-wolf stirs restlessly, drawn to the untamed melody. With a heavy heart, I turn inland, retracing my path under the cathedral arches of the forest. The cloud-veiled moon lights my way back to the dacha. I pause at the edge of the woods, casting one long look over my snowy domain. A wolf's realm.

Soon, I will retreat into the shelter of weathered boards and a smoldering stove. The wild white wolf will slip back into the shadows, ceding her place to the girl in her threadbare coat. But we are one and the same. And when the moon rides high again, we will run unfettered once more through the pale blue night.

I turn to leave the forest's edge when a faint scent catches on the wind—rich and earthy, yet edged with the sharp tang of blood. My wolf's ears prick, a whimper escaping her throat unbidden. She tries to cast about for the source, but I force her onward with a low growl. Whatever poor creature lies dying out there, we cannot help it.

Let's get out of here, girl. Now!

Yet as we near the dacha, the compelling fragrance only grows stronger. My wolf whines pitifully, fixated on locating the injured being. She presses insistently against my will, her curiosity overwhelming.

With a frustrated huff, I relent and let her take control, following the bloody scent north across the snowfields.

The smell leads us to the cliffs above the frozen lake. Through the swirling snow, I spot a dark shape crumpled near the precipice. Man, not beast. Fear spikes through me, but my wolf is deaf to my pleas to turn back. She trots ahead heedlessly, the man's scent enveloping us, thick and cloying.

He lies face down in the snow, one arm flung out limply. Fresh blood stains the ice beneath him a sinister crimson. My thundering pulse drowns out the howling wind as I slowly step nearer. The wolf's curiosity wars with the woman's fear within me. I should flee this place, yet I am transfixed. What tragic twist of fate left this soul stranded and dying in this unforgiving wilderness?

The man stirs faintly, unaware of my presence. My sharp eyes trace over his massive frame, clad all in black. Dark hair whips about his face, obscuring his features.

I stand frozen, only paces away, as the first flecks of a new squall begin to swirl down from the clouds. The scent of blood hangs heavy in the air between us. My two selves clash and waver—woman and wolf, fear and fascination. But as the wind rises into a banshee's scream, drowning out all else, a choice must be made. And on this night, beneath this merciless moon... the wolf wins out.

6

VLAD

Darkness engulfs me. The icy chill of the snow beneath me steals what little warmth remains in my wrecked body. I welcome the numbness, preferring it to the searing agony that wracked me earlier. Perhaps this is how death comes—not in fire and blood, but cradled gently in winter's black arms.

Time fades into meaningless oblivion. I drift, suspended between consciousness and endless night. No scent or sound penetrates the void. Have I crossed into the shadows, at last, my soul detached fully from mortal burdens? Or does my ruined shell yet cling stubbornly to its tether? I cannot tell. I cannot summon the will to care.

Sensation returns slowly. First, the bone-deep ache throbbing heavily in my limbs. Then, the wet rasp of breath sawing in and out of my lungs. So, I do still live—though likely not for long. The functions of this borrowed flesh yet persist against all odds, refusing to still. A growl rumbles in my throat, low and weak. Even on the brink of death, the wolf in me stubbornly fights on.

I force my eyelids open with great effort. The blurred white expanse of snowfields fills my vision. It must be near dawn, the eastern sky barely touched with grey behind black pines. I blink slowly, adjusting. Have I lain here all night since the fight? Grisha still lives, and hunts my brother. But I could not move even if I wished to. My shattered body will not rise again. This lonely wilderness will be my grave.

A shadow passes before me, a silent specter against the ghostly snow. I tense, expecting a killing blow to end this agony. But nothing touches me. Blinking the ice from my lashes, I make out a hulking white shape drawing cautiously nearer. A wolf, with fur the pristine white of a first winter's snow. A hallucination born of blood loss and fading hope. But it seems real enough, moon-bright eyes fixed unblinkingly upon me.

The wolf paces a slow circle around my prostrate form, surveying my injuries with an uncannily intent gaze. This mystical creature's eyes burn with a strange purpose that I cannot grasp. It hesitates, wavering, battling some internal conflict unknown to me. Then finally, it creeps nearer until its face looms directly over mine, warm breath fanning across my cheek.

Gently, it nuzzles along my jawline, the contact sending a spark of warmth through my benumbed nerves. The creature's ministrations grow bolder as I do not resist, licking the congealing blood from my mangled shoulder. The rough caress stings, yet it begins to rouse me from my stupor. I lift my head slightly with a low whine, watching as it moves to lap gingerly at the wounds coating my back and flank.

Why does it help me, a stranger and trespasser in these parts? A dozen questions swirl weakly through my fading mind. But I lack even the strength to voice them. The wolf's gleaming white fur blurs as my head sinks heavily back into the snow. A whimper catches in my throat, animal and human at once. I do not wish to die alone. Not here, so far from Pack and Kin.

The wolf exhales harshly through its nostrils, the almost wolfish equivalent of a resigned sigh. Then its body settles against my uninjured side, a living fur bulwark guarding me against the chill. Its warmth slowly seeps into my bones, kindling a fragile ember of life beneath my endless cold. Its head rests atop mine and lets loose a crystalline howl that rings out defiantly against the silent trees.

I'm here, it proclaims. *You do not walk this path alone.*

Those notes of song are the last thing I know before darkness reclaims me. But this time, its embrace is gentler, cradling, rather than crushing. I surrender willingly, too weary to resist. In fleeting moments between oblivion, I sometimes feel the steady rise and fall of the wolf's flank against me, anchoring me to this world. Our combined heart-beats thrum against the frozen earth—the wolf's strong and relentless, mine ever more hesitant and stumbling. But still, I cling.

I do not know how much time crawls by in fitful bouts of consciousness pierced by nothingness. The sky overhead slowly fades from black to muted grey, heralding the dawn that I did not expect to see. And yet the wolf remains, keeping silent vigil even as night's shadows retreat.

I shift weakly, limbs heavy and aching, but func-tional. The wolf raises its head, eyes gleaming as they meet my own. In them, I see my own reflection—a haggard man, limbs matted with blood and snow, but very much alive. Thanks to its care.

Gratitude wells within my chest, even as questions continue to churn. But before I can voice them, sweet oblivion wraps me in its arms, and this time, there's no fight left in me.

7

VLAD

I awake to shadows. For long moments, I lie still, senses straining against the darkness. Where am I? No familiar scents surround me—only aged wood, melting snow, and the smoky tang of a dying fire. The roar of the storm outside is deafening, even through the walls. I try to rise, only to be met with blinding pain as agony rips through my shoulder and right leg. *Broken. Useless.* A ragged snarl tears from my throat.

Blinking hard, I take stock of my surroundings. A small bed tucked against rough-hewn walls. Moth-eaten wool blankets covering my battered body... As my vision clears, the memories come flooding back—Grisha's savage fangs tearing into my flesh, Luciana's screams as she plummeted to her death.

I shut my eyes against the visceral visions, but still, they hound me. My pulse pounds as I relive every agonizing moment of my failure and loss. Luciana, my brother's mate, sacrificed because I could not protect her. And Gavriil, still missing, his fate hanging maddeningly beyond my reach.

Tears blur my vision unbidden. In letting the traitor Grisha deceive me, I have failed my clan and my pack. My presence was worse than useless in that clearing—it led those I love to harm and death. Never have I felt so hollowed out, so unworthy of the Alpha title I strove so hard to attain.

I remember the mysterious white wolf finding me last night after the fight, its warmth and presence pulling me back from the brink… Was it real? Did I imagine it? Perhaps the wolf spirit's visit confirmed my inadequacy, forsaking me now as punishment.

A bone-deep shame settles over me, more crippling than any physical wound. I am broken in ways no healer can mend. The bandages that dress my wounds may knit my ruined body, but my spirit is a ravaged battlefield no one can salvage. I am lost, adrift, severed from the driving purpose that once defined me.

I start. My heightened hearing picks up the faintest sound of distant movement. Whose home is this? Someone brought me here, wherever *here* may be.

I strain my ears over the gale's cry. There—footsteps, barely audible. Drawing steadily nearer before stopping just outside the closed door. I tense, lifting my head towards the sound despite the pull of bruised muscles. Is it friend or foe beyond that barrier? I brace for a fight, though in my current state, even a single human could end me. My nails extend into claws, ready to tear out the throat of any who dare threaten me.

The door swings inward and I freeze. A young woman stands haloed in firelight, clad only in a simple linen shift. Wary brown eyes meet mine from beneath waves of dark mahogany hair. By her racing heart, she is as uncertain of me as I am of her.

"You're awake," she says bluntly. My heart kicks faster in response. Her voice is pure melody.

I try to rise, to show strength, but a jagged bolt of pain spears my shoulder. I collapse back with a snarl, curses boiling uselessly in my throat.

The woman sits nearby, surveying my struggle with displeasure. Her eyes reflect the low flames flickering in the hearth.

I lick my cracked lips, trying to find my voice.

"What... what happened? Where am I?" The words scrape painfully past my raw throat.

"You were injured, unconscious. I brought you here to recover." Her tone makes it clear she finds the situation an unwelcome inconvenience.

Unease twists my stomach into knots. Anything could have happened while I was locked in oblivion. And this stoic stranger clearly has little incentive to offer aid from genuine kindness. I must get my bearings and assess whether she poses a threat. But for now, I am trapped here at her mercy.

Again, I try to sit up, to take stock of my body's damage. But my mangled shoulder and splinted leg scream in protest. A roar builds in my chest.

"Don't." The woman's voice cracks sharply through the haze of pain. "Please, don't tamper with your wound dressings. It'll mess up the healing process."

My answering growl holds both agony and indignation. Who is she to tell me what I may or may not do? I am no helpless cub or dotard elder. I am Vladimir Volkov, Alpha of the Roman wolf pack. Or was, before shame and failure stripped that title from me.

The woman steps further into the cramped room, movements cautious. She stops a safe distance away, head angled warily. "Do you have a name?" she asks after an extended silence.

I grunt, still battling the fire in my wounds. "Vlad... Vladimir," I finally grind out. She nods slowly, considering. Her next words are so soft I almost miss them.

"I'm Anya."

Anya. The name whispers through my mind, tangled with glimpses of white fur and patient vigil. I can't stop thinking of the lone wolf that kept me from death's door... Exhaustion plays tricks on me. I don't know *what* to believe, who to trust, or what my future holds.

Anya meets my stare levelly, betraying nothing of her own thoughts. But her quickened pulse and flare of scent—pine and wild musk, mingled with light floral notes—reveal an apprehension she masks well. What is she afraid of? Me?

"Alright, Vlad," Anya says briskly, shattering the heavy silence. "I brought you some food. You should eat." She turns and retrieves a steaming bowl from the cluttered table, bringing it over to set on the night-stand within my reach. The savory aroma of meat broth fills my nose, reminding me how long it's been since I've properly fed. But wariness stays my hand.

Anya straightens, fixing me with a piercing look.

"We'll talk in a bit," she says curtly, then retreats from the room, shutting me in alone again with my doubts.

I eye the offered meal, torn between hunger and suspicion. Can I trust this mysterious girl not to poison me while I lie helpless in her den? But no—if she meant ill, why heal me at all? Why not abandon me to die in the snowy field? I take up the bowl with my good hand, sloshing the simple broth. My empty stomach outweighs caution. I swallow every drop, licking the bowl clean, before collapsing back onto the lumpy mattress.

Sleep tugs at my weakened body, urging me to drift back into dark oblivion where pain cannot follow. But questions still plague me, denying any real rest.

Slipping in and out of consciousness, I do not know how much time has passed. The fire wanes to sullen coals in the soot-stained hearth. Anya does not return. I begin to wonder if she was even real at all, or just another fever dream. But I can still detect her moonlit scent if I focus... pine boughs, wild musk, layered with sweet peony and woven with my own. Proof of her presence, however fleeting.

At length, footsteps sound again outside, followed by the scrape of the door opening. Anya slips in soundlessly. Our eyes meet in silence weighted by uncertainty. She claimed we would talk, but where does one begin unraveling the strangeness that binds us?

"How are you feeling?" Anya asks eventually, still hovering several strides away. Her tone is less brusque now, almost gentle. The change sparks both relief and anger within me. I need no coddling, not even from she who pulled me back from the shadows.

"Well as can be expected," I rasp in reply. Better to not show more weakness.

Anya's eyes track the bandages swathing my injuries, seeing through my bravado. With care, she settles onto the room's lone chair, watching the fitful fire rather than me. She's waiting for me to break the fragile peace with my questions. But I will not grant her that power over me yet. She called this meeting— let *her* be the one to begin unraveling our shared riddle.

The fire pops and hisses as we study one another in the dimness. Anya carries herself with a stillness that seems all too familiar. A fierce capacity for silence and patience not many can muster. But there is anxiety in her studied poise, betraying the calm. She fears what I represent—an intruder into her isolated haven. And with good reason.

At long last, she exhales harshly, shoulders slumping as if in defeat. "Very well. I suppose we should... address the obvious, as much as can be addressed." She pauses, marshaling herself. "You likely have questions. About where you are, who I am. I will answer what I can."

I wet my cracked lips before responding. "I would appreciate that."

She inclines her head in acquiescence. Clasping her hands tightly in her lap, Anya begins haltingly recounting the events following our battlefield encounter.

She confirms that she was gathering wood when she found me bloodied and unconscious in the snow. With great difficulty, she managed to half drag, half carry me here to her secluded home. She mended me as best she was able. Beyond that sparse outline, she provides little additional detail, instead lapsing again into wary silence.

Her tale solves some riddles, yet raises others. "You live here alone?" I prompt into the uneasy stillness. Anya's pulse jumps at my question, but she nods in confirmation.

"For some time now, yes."

"Why?" I do not ask merely to pry, but to unravel any potential threats.

Anya's eyes flash with anger at my bold query. "I could ask the same of you," she retorts coldly. "Why do you wander these parts alone and bloodied, trespassing onto my lands?"

I bristle at her pointed words. The events preceding our crossing are still raw wounds in my mind. Wounds I do not wish to expose to this stranger's scrutiny. Anya seems to sense she overstepped, exhaling heavily as the tension bleeds from her taut frame.

"Forgive me," she murmurs. "It's only... I've grown unaccustomed to having company. Solitude changes us, doesn't it?" Her gaze turns inward, seeing phantoms. "You need not relive troubled memories on my account."

An unpleasant realization strikes me then—she is as much an outcast as I am now. We are two souls severed from their kin, each bearing the scars of that rupture. A harsh fate for anyone—wolf or human. At last, I understand the wary distance Anya keeps between us. She's accustomed to solitude. I too, have guarded my secrets and pain closely since parting ways with the Ursa. Yet if there is any hope of gleaning answers from each other, these barriers must come down.

Swallowing the knot in my throat, I try to piece

together a plausible story to satisfy Anya's questions without revealing my true nature.

"I was attacked by... some kind of wild beast while hiking in these woods," I say slowly. "I don't remember much else. It's still a blur."

Anya's eyes narrow, and I can tell she suspects there is more I'm not saying.

"What kind of beast?" she presses with urgency. "Can you describe it?"

I avoid her probing stare, feigning a dazed confusion. "I'm not sure. It happened so fast, and I struck my head in the struggle. I only recall teeth and claws before everything went dark." I let out a low groan, as if trying to conjure phantom memories.

"Hmm…" Anya murmurs. She leans back in her chair, unconvinced. "Well, I'm sure it will come back to you eventually. The mind has ways of unlocking trauma when it's ready."

I nod vaguely, keeping my face carefully blank. I hate deceiving this woman who saved my life. But revealing my true shifter nature could put her in graver danger. Until I recover my strength, secrecy is my best protection for us both.

Anya seems to sense my unease with her continued questions. With a soft sigh, she rises to stoke the dying fire.

"You should rest," she says gently. "There will be time enough for troubling memories later, once you've healed."

I relax slightly as she turns the subject to my more immediate needs. My identity remains hidden, for now. But her perceptive eyes see more than she admits. I have to be cautious around this woman, or I may reveal more than is wise.

In the dying firelight, something fragile forms between us then—a wordless understanding that requires no further voicing. Two souls, neither whole nor undamaged, finding solace in a kindred spirit. The silence that settles is a comfortable one.

When Anya eventually rises to add a log to the sputtering flames, I do not tense or flinch at her nearness. A curious sensation, trusting one who is still mostly a stranger. But my wolf recognizes her now as more than a mere stranger. *Packmate,* though no formal oaths bind us. Linked by trauma and circumstance. And in the sharing of our wounds, the first steps towards healing have perhaps begun.

I know not what the next day's light will reveal about my own path forward. Whether this sheltered cabin will become a way station on my road, or the endpoint of my ruined quest. But here, now, I feel the stirrings of hope within my battered soul. Hope, and the warmth of a hearth's fire shared with one who understands. It is enough for this night. The rest will come as it always does—one step at a time.

With that consoling thought, I let exhaustion reclaim me at last. Anya's steady presence remains long after slumber steals my waking mind. And this time, no phantoms haunt my dreams. There is only the comfort of pack, of bones and blood and breath shared. It buoys me through the darkness, allowing me true rest.

8

ANYA

I sink down onto the pile of blankets I've laid out on the studio floor, the day's events racing through my mind. It's been mere hours since I stumbled upon the mysterious injured man in the snowdrifts—Vladimir, as he gruffly named himself. Yet somehow, helping him has already disrupted the predictable rhythms of my solitary life.

I'd thought myself inured to loneliness after so long apart from any true pack or companionship. But something in Vlad's stern demeanor calls to me in ways I don't quite understand. My wolf stirs restlessly, fixated on our unexpected houseguest now resting in my bed. She seems to sense some deeper bond between us that my human half cannot grasp.

With a frustrated sigh, I wrap my arms around

myself tightly. This cramped studio holds no hearth, just icy drafts sneaking through warped floorboards. But a chill deeper than the physical cold has worked its way into my bones. Why did I bring this stranger here, into my haven? What fascination made me ignore all caution to save him?

His wounds tell of violence barely survived, hinting at a bloody history. Everything in his manner suggests a dangerous man, hardened and aloof. And yet... the haunted sorrow in his grey eyes when fever claimed him tells another tale. Of tragedies weathered and losses unmourned. It resonated deeply with my own story, in ways I wish it hadn't.

Some naive impulse had me bare my throat to help him, bringing us closer in vulnerability than I've allowed with anyone in years. Just the memory of our conversation now makes my pulse quicken for reasons beyond wariness. Unbidden heat blossoms under my skin despite the frigid air. I squeeze my eyes shut, willing my thoughts away from Vladimir's rugged physique and why it affects me so.

This is madness. I know nothing about him beyond those fleeting glimpses past his defenses. He could be anyone, anything. A wanted man who's committed unspeakable acts. Even a murderer, wandering these desolate hills. For all I know, he has a mate and a whole litter of pups waiting for his return, while I sit here pathetically craving his attention.

A mirthless laugh escapes my tight throat. Listen to me, mooning over a complete stranger as if I stand a chance with someone like *him*. He'll be on his way as soon as he's recovered enough to travel, disappearing from my life as abruptly as he entered it. Better to keep my distance from the rugged stranger currently sleeping in my bed. Safer for both of us.

Scolding myself for foolish flights of fancy, I burrow deeper into the meager blankets and try to quiet my racing mind. But unconsciousness eludes me for long restless hours as winter's wind batters the cabin walls. My thoughts churn too violently, replaying my impulsive choice to save Vladimir, to bring him here. Questioning the unexplainable magnetism that holds me rapt.

Eventually, I slip into disjointed dreams haunted by grey eyes and the memory of his harsh panting breaths mingling with mine as we lay face to face in the bloodstained snow. My last fleeting thoughts before sleep claims me are of fierce wolves running together under the moonlight. Of the piercing joy and terror of the hunt. Then blessed darkness drags me under to more pleasant fantasies where a lonely girl is no longer quite so alone.

Morning arrives in a flood of pale light that makes me wince. Every muscle aches from a long night of tossing and turning on unforgiving wooden planks. I force myself upright, shivering in the biting chill that permeates the studio. Tonight, I will be smarter and stoke the stove's embers to ward off the worst cold. If Vladimir is amenable, perhaps I can even convince him to relocate here while he continues healing. Pride insists I reclaim my bed sooner than later.

First things first, though—I need to check on my unexpected patient. I splash some icy water on my face to banish the last bleariness of broken sleep, then make my way quietly to the bedroom. The door creaks softly as I ease it open, cautiously peering inside.

Vladimir is still deeply unconscious, his big frame barely fitting on my humble bed. But his rest seems peaceful now compared to the earlier delirium. I tiptoe closer, laying a palm on his forehead as I check him over. The fever has broken, leaving only residual warmth and the faintest dewy sweat. He's past the worst danger now. Relief floods through me—the last thing I need is to have a dead guy in my cabin in the middle of a snowstorm.

Sensing my presence on some instinctive level,

Vlad stirs and turns his head towards me. Eyes still shut, he nuzzles into my touch like a contented wolf. My breath catches at the unexpectedly tender gesture. Has he mistaken me in his half-conscious state for someone else he actually knows and trusts? The thought brings an odd tightness to my chest.

I start to withdraw my hand, but Vladimir's own comes up to capture it before I can pull away. His thickly callused fingers engulf mine as he holds me there a moment longer, the contact sending an electric spark arcing through my skin. I freeze, stunned by the intensity of sensation from such an innocent touch. Eyes still closed, he inhales deeply as though fixing my scent to memory.

Oh, sweet Moon Goddess… Fuck!

"Stay..." he rasps, voice slurred by sleep. He tugs gently, coaxing me down to perch on the bed's edge. Dumbstruck, I let him draw me closer as his breathing evens out again. Soon, his grip on my hand goes lax. But I find myself unable to break free, unwilling to disturb this unexpected intimacy.

My inner wolf keens joyfully, reveling in our linked hands and his warmth so near. Traitorous woman that I am, I cannot deny a similar rightness in this simple contact. My instincts howl to curl up beside this wounded brute and offer what comfort I can. To lay my head on that broad chest and listen to the steady beat of his great heart.

I know I should pull away, leave this room before I'm drawn any deeper into Vladimir's unpredictable orbit. But never have I felt more torn between duty and desire. Would allowing myself to indulge in this small affection really be so dangerous? Perhaps this stranger will depart soon and leave my well-ordered world unchanged. And so, I remain seated vigilantly beside him as morning stretches towards afternoon. Watching the steady rise and fall of his chest, our fingers loosely entwined like old friends. Or even lovers.

Dangerous, foolish thoughts. I repeat the warnings in my head like a mantra, though they do little to drown out my reckless longing. This man is not my mate or companion. Only a happenstance guest, his stay fleeting. I would do well to remember that, no matter how the she-wolf inside me whines and begs.

Still... I make no move to disentangle our hands as Vladimir slumbers on. Craving even this faint connection for just a little while longer.

9

VLAD

’m lost in a captivating fantasy, my hands tangled in Anya’s silken mahogany hair. Our lips crash together urgently, hers so incredibly warm and soft against my own. She tastes of honey and whispered secrets. My wolf howls triumphantly, craving more of her addictive sweetness.

I trail hungry kisses down the elegant column of her throat, feeling her racing pulse under my tongue. Her quiet gasps and sighs of pleasure intoxicate me. I nip at the tender skin just above her collarbone, needing to mark her, claim her as mine. Anya arches into me, fingers digging into my shoulders, silently begging for more.

My hands roam her lithe form, tracing each curve through her thin linen shift. I break our kiss to nuzzle the valley between her breasts, inhaling the floral scent that's been driving my wolf to the brink of madness. Anya's breath hitches, lashes fluttering. She guides my mouth back to hers and I'm lost again, drowning in her heat.

Oh, gods. We shouldn't. Not yet... But my willpower dissolves against the onslaught of desire, the ferocious need to bond with this exquisite creature in every way. Anya seems just as lost, her kisses growing more insistent. I must have her, make her fully mine, fate and propriety be damned.

I trail my kiss along her sharp jawline to the sensitive spot beneath her ear. "Say you're mine," I demand hoarsely.

Anya moans, surrendering to my touch. And then, her lips part briefly to answer...

"Vladimir?"

Anya's melodic voice pierces the haze of desire. I blink awake, the dream fading as morning light filters into the cramped bedroom. She sits at my bedside, regarding me curiously.

"Time to change your dressings," she says briskly, though twin spots of color bloom on her cheekbones. Does she guess the nature of my fevered visions? Shame flushes through me. She's not mine to fantasize about, no matter how my lonely wolf might ache for her.

Clearing my throat, I struggle to sit up with Anya's help. Her nearness makes my pulse race anew, the phantom taste of her lips still tingling on my tongue. I force myself to be still as she carefully unwinds the bandages swaddling my wounds. But my hungry gaze traces the elegant line of her throat, recalling how I kissed and nipped that tender skin in my unrestrained dream.

A low rumble escapes my chest before I can prevent it. Anya's eyes widen at the sound, her own breath quickening. Does she also feel this electric draw between us, as if we're connected by some deeper bond?

I clench my fists, fighting the urge to pull her against me. She is not mine to take such liberties with. But the wolf within whines and paces, craving her nearness.

Anya looks up at me through dark lashes. "Is something wrong?" Her voice is husky, uncertain.

I shake my head mutely, not trusting my own ragged voice. We stare at each other, the air suddenly charged.

With a soft inhale, Anya turns back to her task,

the facade of composure back in place. "Let's get these dressings changed, shall we?"

I nod, pulse racing as her hands gently peel away the bandages swaddling my wounds. Her touches seem lighter than before, almost tentative. Does she intuit how she affects me? I dare not hope I might stir a similar longing in her.

I sit perfectly still, studying her lowered face intently. Delicate brows knot in concentration, teeth worrying her full lower lip. A wayward lock of mahogany hair spills over her cheek and my fingers itch to brush it back, to feel if her skin is as smooth and warm as it appears.

I clench my traitorous hand, tamping down the instinct. Anya has been unfailingly gracious, taking me in and nursing me back from death's door. I will not repay that kindness by presuming any unwelcome familiarity. No matter how this waifish girl intrigues me, with her contradictory mix of timidity and quiet strength.

Anya's nimble fingers work slowly along my arm, revealing the stylized wolves inked there. "Oh… Do you like wolves?" she asks abruptly, tracing one outlined form. My breath catches at the contact, even that simple graze kindling sparks beneath my skin.

I master my features to stillness, cursing my wolf's

predictable reaction to her nearness. "I do," I answer neutrally, hoping my voice does not betray my quickened pulse. This is unwise, dangerous. If she guesses what I am, the tentative trust between us could unravel in an instant.

Oblivious to my inner turmoil, Anya just nods. "That's nice." She withdraws her hand and my arm feels suddenly cold without her touch. I flex my fingers involuntarily, craving her warmth again, even knowing I should keep my distance. But this girl has stirred something reckless in me, an irresistible pull like gravity, inescapable.

"Do *you*?" I ask, needing to keep her talking, to learn more of what lurks behind those fathomless dark eyes.

Anya busies herself tidying the medical supplies, avoiding my stare. "Sometimes," she says evasively.

My instincts bristle at her reticence. She hides something beneath that timid facade. Is it mere shyness... or deeper secrets? The mysteries surrounding Anya only increase my fascination.

But who am I to pry and demand she bare herself fully to a stranger? The gods know I have my own share of shadows best left undisturbed.

Anya owes me no explanation for the choices that led her to isolation in this wilderness. Perhaps in time, trust will grow between us, and she will share her past unburdened. But only if and when she herself deems it right. I must be patient if I wish to truly earn passage beyond those wary defenses.

For now, I will let her keep her silence, and her secrets. Anya has already proven herself generous and compassionate simply by taking me in. I can ask no more of her than that—and hope my actions might eventually show I am worthy of the same grace in kind. If fate wills us to reveal our hearts, let it unfold at its own pace.

Anya continues to work in silence. I'm amazed at how much the wounds have improved overnight—the angry red gashes now knitted into scabbed-over lines. At this rate, I should be ready to resume my hunt for Grisha sooner than expected.

"Remarkable," she murmurs, brows furrowing as she inspects the accelerated healing. "Looks like you'll be good as new in no time."

I just nod, unwilling to reveal my kind's rapid regenerative powers. Anya repacks her medical supplies, then glances towards the frosted window.

"The storm seems to be letting up," she says. "It was fierce all through the night—I'm sure you heard the wind howling."

"Oh, yeah… definitely," I reply awkwardly. "Kept me up a while… all that howling and stuff."

I resist the urge to wince. *Smooth. Real smooth, Vlad.* Something about Anya reduces me to a blundering adolescent, completely tongue-tied. Where's my usual charm and confidence?

If Anya notices my fumbling reply, she's kind enough not to show it. "Well, I'll be in my studio if you need anything. No TV or internet out here, I'm afraid. Just books and my art to pass the time."

She gathers the soiled bandages and moves towards the door. "Don't hesitate to call for me, alright?"

With an aborted half-wave, Anya exits hastily, leaving me alone to ponder my unusual flustered reactions to her presence. I've faced down vicious enemies and seductive temptresses without breaking a sweat. So what spell has this unassuming girl cast to unravel my composure so completely? I fear finding the answer may upend everything I thought I knew about myself.

10

ANYA

I kept the conversation pragmatic as I unwrapped Vlad's healing gashes, clinically assessing his progress. He remained still and stoic throughout, responding minimally to my prompts. Only the occasional tightening of his jaw betrayed any discomfort as I touched the swollen flesh and realigned his splints. His skin was warm under my hands, threaded with scars that speak of a violent history. I focused only on treating the wounds before me, ignoring the flush creeping up my cheeks or my quickened pulse.

Mercifully, Vlad made no mention of the charged atmosphere brewing between us. Once I finished tending his injuries, he murmured a sincere word of thanks and then excused himself to rest, perhaps sensing my unsettled state. I eased out a breath as my quiet footsteps trailed down the hall and the strange tension in the air finally began dissipating.

I was anything but impressed by his quick recovery, despite my feigned surprise. I knew the *real* reason behind it—my wolf's healing powers when she licked his wounds clean on that fateful night. But I couldn't risk revealing my abilities to Vlad, or he would surely uncover my true identity. So I put on a show of astonishment, while secretly urging his body to continue mending swiftly, thanks to the lasting effects of my hidden efforts.

By all the gods and the Moon Goddess herself, what is happening to me? I have survived this long by maintaining utmost control—over my solitary domain, my closely guarded secrets, and my own emotions. Yet this stranger's arrival has breached the formidable walls I built to hold the world at bay, stirring up chaotic feelings I do not understand. I need the clarity of my wolf, the purity of animal instinct unclouded by human complexities. I need to run, to be wild and unfettered under the moon's eye once more.

But I can't. The blizzard's fury still rages beyond these choked eaves. For now, I remain caged, alone with my canvases and an enigmatic injured man who draws forth such troublesome reactions from the woman and the she-wolf within me. Until the storm passes, I can only brew herbs to calm my restless mind and paint the hours away, losing myself in the familiar haven of creation.

Picking up my abandoned brush, I add a dash of crimson to the nameless wolf's fur, kindling a ruddy fire beneath her moonlit pelt. An improvement, but the life in her gaze remains trapped behind the veil of paint and varnish. She is only ever a shadow of the creature I become under the stars. A copy of a copy, each step removed from truth diminishing the spirit a little more.

No, this is not the answer I seek. With a muffled curse, I fling the defective canvas aside. It cracks against the far wall, streaking the faded planks with paint. Chest heaving, I drop my head into hands that reek of turpentine. I cannot capture the wild on canvas. I cannot outrun this nameless longing clawing inside. I cannot escape the maelstrom this stranger Vlad has awakened within me.

For good or ill, I must accept that my world will never be the same again. Once the storm breaks, our paths will diverge and he will vanish from my solitary life as suddenly as he entered it. All I can do is weather the strange days that remain between now and then, however taxing they prove.

The inner whirlwind cannot be calmed by calculated reason. But it can be endured—with patience over passion, pragmatism over intensity of feeling. I must cling to the lessons that have kept me safe all these seasons in the wilderness.

And perhaps, before this trial ends, the she-wolf and I will finally understand why our logic failed us that moonlit night... the night we heard the call of the pack once more in a broken howl and found ourselves helpless but to answer.

Sighing, I tidy up my art supplies and set a fresh canvas on the easel. I need a productive distraction from the chaotic thoughts about the alluring stranger now under my roof.

Loading my palette with paints, I begin roughing out the outlines of a snowy Saint Petersburg scene—specifically the beautiful Bridge of Kisses over the Moika River. I sketch in the graceful ironwork arches and gilded embellishments of the bridge's railings, all dusted white with fresh snowfall.

In the background, I lightly pencil in the pastel outlines of the surrounding historic buildings along the embankment. The intricate facades reflect softly in the icy waters of the partially frozen river below the bridge.

Yulia will be thrilled when she sees this romantic river scene. Whimsical urban landscapes are always in high demand from her hotel clients. I have three weeks to capture all the delicate details of the bridge's ornate metalwork and paint one more wintry Saint Petersburg cityscape.

But as I start to block in the architecture, adding soft blues to the canvas, my traitorous mind keeps wandering away from the familiar sights of my old hometown.

My wolf stirs restlessly, fixated on our new house-guest. She prods me to go to him, insisting some deeper bond exists between us. But I dismiss the reckless notions. Vladimir likely has a whole life waiting for him back home, wherever that may be. He's not meant for me.

With a low growl of frustration, I dash more blue onto my canvas, trying to lose myself in the work. But Vlad's stormy eyes and sculpted physique haunt my thoughts, distracting me from painting.

I can perfectly envision his ruggedly handsome features—strong jawline darkened by stubble, raven hair falling carelessly over his brow. And his body... even wounded, Vlad radiates raw power and masculine grace. I've traced the hard contours of his muscular chest and arms while tending his injuries, felt them tense and flex beneath my hands.

Heat rises in my cheeks remembering the thrill his nearness provoked, my dizzying awareness of him as a man, not merely a patient. The intoxicating scent of his skin—cedar smoke and mountain air—lingers in my memory. As does the allure of danger and dominance he exudes, so different from the safe detachment of my solitary life.

Everything about him seems designed to tempt me, from those piercing grey eyes to his deep, rumbling voice that makes my pulse flutter helplessly. What would it be like to be enveloped in those strong arms, pressed close against such a commanding figure? To have the full force of his focus fixed solely on me? The reckless fantasies keep invading my carefully ordered thoughts, spurred on by my she-wolf's wanton cravings.

With an effort, I wrench my mind back to the canvas before me. I came in here to seek clarity and purpose, not mooning over a captivating stranger who will soon be gone from my reality...

This fixation is useless, I scold myself harshly. Vladimir will be gone soon, disappeared from my life as abruptly as he entered it. I must keep my distance, guard my heart. Yet even as my rational mind knows this truth, my she-wolf continues to pace and whine for his nearness.

If only this snowstorm would cease, allowing our lives to diverge once more. But we remain caged here a while longer, two restless souls churning with unspoken thoughts. This strange new tension is our reality now. However taxing, all I can do is endure it with patience... and pray my defenses hold firm against this growing storm within.

11

ANYA

’m dragged reluctantly from sleep by the pale winter light filtering through the studio’s frosted windowpanes, casting everything in shades of muted blue. Blinking blearily, I lift my head from where I slumped over on my worktable. The unfinished Saint Petersburg cityscape mocks me from the easel—seems I passed out mid-brushstroke last night.

Judging by the weak sunlight, it must be late morning already. I stretch my stiff limbs, wincing at the crick in my neck from dozing at such an odd angle all night. This cramped studio was not meant for sleeping, but I couldn’t bring myself to return to the bedroom I’ve given over to Vlad. Just the thought of him makes my pulse quicken, remnants of hazy dreams stirring.

A heavy exhaustion clings to my bones despite the long rest, evidence of my inner turmoil. My demanding wolf does not understand why I keep avoiding our handsome wounded guest. She paces back and forth, her whining incessant, craving his company, his touch. But their forbidden allure terrifies me. I cannot trust my reactions when Vlad is near, as yesterday proved. Far safer to keep my distance until he's gone.

Outside, the storm has finally exhausted its fury, though venturing out into the lingering blizzard would still be madness. It seems Vlad and I will continue to be trapped here for a little longer, pushing my self-restraint to its limits.

With a resigned sigh, I dip my brush in brilliant azure paint and half-heartedly add a few clean strokes to the frozen river beneath the Bridge of Kisses. But concentration eludes me, my mind fogged by weariness and unsettled thoughts.

A knock at the studio door jolts me from my artistic trance and nearly makes me tip over my paint water. I set down my brush, pulse quickening with anticipation and unease. There's only one other soul currently taking shelter within these walls.

"Come in," I call, keeping my voice carefully neutral. The door creaks open to reveal Vlad's imposing figure filling the doorway. I sit frozen, paintbrush dripping unheeded as my exhausted brain struggles to reconcile the man before me with the one haunting my dreams all night.

His dark hair is disheveled and his eyes bleary from sleep. The splints on his leg are gone, and he seems to be putting some weight on it now. He looks far stronger today, some color returned to his rugged features. The silk shirt he wears strains slightly over his chest, revealing enticing glimpses of smooth tanned skin and hard muscle. My mouth goes dry, inner wolf keening wantonly at the prime masculine specimen now watching me with stormy eyes.

He scans the cluttered studio curiously before his gaze settles on my work in progress. Something complex flashes through his expression then. Surprise? Affinity? Fear? I cannot decipher it fully before his stony mask slides back into place.

"Hey," I offer gently, trying to set him at ease. "I hope you slept alright."

"Well enough, thanks to your hospitality." His voice is a soft rumble, though I can still detect traces of his earlier guardedness.

"Apologies if I interrupted you," Vlad murmurs.

His deep voice rolls through me, leaving exquisite tingles in its wake. "I thought you might like some tea..."

Tea. Of course. I try to gather some shred of poise, clearing my sleep-roughened throat. "Sure. I'll just go prepare some—"

"It's not a request," Vlad interjects, tone abruptly curt. I freeze, eyes widening. He seems to realize his sharpness and softens his voice. "What I mean is... I've already made it. I wished to do this small thing for you, as thanks for your care these past days."

Heat blooms in my cheeks at the gentle reprimand. "Oh... That's very kind of you, Vlad. Please, come in."

I make to stand on still-unsteady legs but Vlad is there in an instant, setting down the tea tray to gently grip my shoulder. "No need to get up on my account," he murmurs, gray eyes crinkling with smile lines. "Relax. You've more than earned it after caring for me so selflessly."

His light hold feels scorching even through my wool sweater. I can only nod numbly as Vlad releases me to prepare our tea, my skin prickling at the lingering sensation of his fingers branding my flesh. I want those hands on me again, stroking, claiming... *No, stop.* I force the reckless imaginings down, watching mutely as Vlad makes himself at home in my private creative space.

Soon, we sit facing each other. The tea is bold and fragrant, its earthy flavor finally rousing me fully awake. Vlad watches me over the curling steam, content to sit without speaking. But the heavy silence only amplifies the charged air. I fidget under his intense stare, pulse racing. Does he also feel this nameless magnetism steadily drawing us together?

Clearing my throat, I make stilted small talk to fill the expectant hush. "The storm seems to finally be moving on. But it still looks treacherous out there..."

Vlad's eyes crinkle again in that unfairly attractive way. "No need to rush. I'm more than happy to enjoy your gracious hospitality a while longer." His deep timbre caresses the words, sending traitorous shivers racing down my spine.

I can sense his eyes tracking me, taking in my home with a dominant assessing gaze… What must he see as he studies these cramped and faded spaces? The trappings of a hermit's life, barren of any real comfort or joy? I find I do not wish for this stranger to view me solely as an object of pity, even if the assumption is understandable.

"It's not much, I know. But it suits me well enough." I keep my tone light as Vlad hands me a steaming cup. Our fingers brush briefly, and the spark of contact kindles a flutter low in my belly that catches me off guard. I pull back swiftly, disguising my surprise. *What was that?* A mere accident, nothing more.

We sip our tea in pensive silence as dawn's light strengthens beyond the windows. My thoughts keep returning to that odd pang of awareness from our chance touch, probing it for meaning. This man is still largely a mystery to me, one I have opened my door to but not my heart to. I cannot explain my wolf's urgency in dragging his battered form out of the darkness—or the way her fascination has bled over to tinge my own human perceptions as well.

The details of Vlad's violent history may remain obscure, but his hardened physique and self-contained intensity leave little doubt that he has long walked in savage territories. His is a strong spirit, burned and honed by suffering into something powerful yet broken. Everything in his manner suggests he is unused to relying on others... or freely trusting anyone beyond himself. I suspect he finds the vulnerability of convalescence here galling, no matter my assurances of welcome.

And yet, beneath that stern exterior, I sense flashes of a kinder soul—one who mourns loss deeply, takes blows hard, and desperately craves connection. One who would be gentle with beloved friends, though merciless towards enemies.

In our brief interactions, he has revealed little of his inner self. But I find I wish to learn more, to solve the riddle of what hardens him... and what wounds him. My she-wolf stirs with unease, equally drawn by this enigmatic stranger in our midst.

Abruptly, I realize Vlad is studying me in turn, perhaps reading the pensiveness on my face. I drop my gaze, a flush creeping up my neck. How long has he been observing me while my mind wandered? What untold thoughts might show in my features?

An awkward silence swells between us. I clutch my cooling cup of tea just for something to do with my suddenly trembling hands. Vlad seems content to sit and scrutinize me a while longer, no hint of his own thoughts in those fathomless grey eyes.

12
VLAD

Needing to dispel this electric tension, I rise swiftly to pace the cramped room. What is the matter with me? I'm trying real hard not to act a fool around Anya, but one look from those big doe eyes and I'm back to square one—tripping over my own tongue like a blundering schoolboy.

I try to keep our interactions light and courteous, sincerely concerned for her well-being as my care-taker. But my voice always comes out too gruff, words sharp as gravel. Curse it all. I'm usually quite charming, effortlessly navigating social nuance. Yet somehow, that talent fails me completely in this girl's presence.

Anya makes me feel off-balance in ways no seductress or battlefield has ever managed—and she likely has no idea of the effect she has on me. I'm torn between fascination with this waifish artist and frustration at my fumbling reactions. I survived the harshest winters and bloodiest wars through discipline and ironclad control. So, how can one wounded young woman unravel my hard-won composure so easily?

Perhaps the head injury I sustained has rattled me more than I realized. Surely, that must explain these strange obsessive thoughts circling Anya no matter how I try to dismiss them. Why I find myself dreaming of her velvet brown eyes and chestnut hair fanned across my chest as we...

Abruptly, I halt my aimless pacing, cursing under my breath. There it is again—reckless imaginings creeping in completely unbidden. I drag a hand roughly across my face, as though I can physically wipe away the heated memories. *Control yourself, man. Anya deserves respect, not crude fantasies.*

Squaring my shoulders, I decide to stride out of the cramped studio before my traitorous thoughts can continue down dangerous paths. I need a bracing breath of crisp air to clear my muddled head. Away from Anya's distracting proximity, surely reason can reassert some mastery over my unruly impulses. With patience and distance, I can weather this strange fixation until it passes. Can't I?

Dull pain flares in my leg as I head outside, but I grit my teeth against it. Anya's head jerks up, features creasing in renewed worry. She startles at the noise when I brace myself against the doorjamb.

"You shouldn't be walking like that," she says, her soft words pinning me in place. "I think your leg is broken."

I test my weight gingerly. "It's not," I state bluntly. In truth, the bone has already fused back together with preternatural swiftness. Lingering soreness slows me, but the strength has returned.

Anya's brows knit together skeptically. "That's impossible. I felt the fracture myself two days ago. Come to think of it, you should be bedbound still."

I shrug, feigning ignorance. "Perhaps it was just a bad sprain. I'm a fast healer." Let her make of that what she will, so long as she does not guess the unnatural cause. Seeming unconvinced, Anya opens her mouth to argue but I cut her off.

"So, uh… you're an artist." I gesture at the half-finished canvases propped around us, eager to redirect the conversation. If I can keep her off-balance, she will have less opportunity to scrutinize me too closely.

"I wouldn't say that," Anya mumbles, picking at

her stained apron self-consciously. "But, yes. I paint a little."

I move slowly among her works, examining the wintry scenes comprising her modest portfolio. "Are these all yours?"

She nods, discomfort growing at having her creations so openly appraised. I pause at a small piece depicting a snow-laden pine forest. It strikes some deep chord within me, cherished yet forlorn.

"These are beautiful," I murmur. "This one reminds me of my childhood."

The snow-capped pines and icy river could be transplants from the ancient forests surrounding Saint Petersburg, where I spent my early years. I see the shining palace in the distance, the sweeping neoclassical facade where my family, the formidable Alexeev Ursa clan, still keeps ancestral lands and property.

Unthinking, I reach out to trace the evocative brushstrokes that vividly capture a landscape from my most distant memories. I recall playing in the snowy courtyards with my younger brother Gavriil, our pealing laughter and rapid footsteps chasing away the heavy silence that blanketed those grand halls. We were rambunctious and inseparable then, two cubs roaming our domain without a care—not the Alpha youths of decades later, battling to outshine each other, always in constant competition.

As I run my fingers over the textured oil paint, pain instantly lances through my wounded shoulder at the careless motion, jolting me rudely back to the present. I stifle a hiss between clenched teeth as the sweet nostalgia sours in a heartbeat. Those golden days were long ago, turned to ash by tragedy and betrayal. Now Gavriil lies broken, and I am a defeated outcast, far from home. The gulf between past and present has never felt more acute, more biting.

Anya rushes to my side, gently steering me towards the room's lone chair. "You should lie down," she frets. "I think I have some painkillers in the kitchen."

She takes a step forward but hesitates, glancing between me and the hallway beyond. "I'll go check."

As she turns to leave, my roving gaze lands on the rumpled blankets piled in the corner—a makeshift bed that can only be Anya's. I frown, piecing together the truth.

"Wait," I call out, my voice harsher than I intended. Anya stills but keeps her back to me. "Have you been sleeping here this whole time?"

Her slim shoulders hunch slightly. "It's alright, really," she mumbles dismissively.

I stand swiftly, ignoring the spike of pain the motion causes. "No, it's not. You gave up your bed for me. That's not right." I step closer, suddenly desperate to remedy this unfairness. "You should take it back. The studio floor will be enough for me."

Anya finally faces me, skepticism plain in her delicate features. "Seriously? Look at you—you're injured. You need the bed more than I do."

I cross my arms, resolve hardening my expression. "I won't rest easy knowing you're reduced to this for my sake."

Anya fixes me with a piercing stare. "What exactly are you suggesting?"

Reckless words spill from my lips before reason can rein me in. "We could share the bed."

Anya's cheeks bloom crimson. She opens her mouth only to snap it shut, at a loss.

I press on in the loaded silence. "Look. It's practical," I assure her. "The bed looks large enough for two."

Anya finds her voice, at last, flustered. "That's... a generous offer. But I couldn't possibly..."

Refusing to retract my hasty offer, I tilt my chin up defiantly. "Then it's settled. We'll share the bed starting tonight."

I brush past Anya's stunned form and gather up

her makeshift bedding from the corner. Frozen in shock, she makes no move to stop me as I stride purposefully into the hall.

What have I done? How the hell will I be able to resist her? My wolf has been screaming for me to claim her from the moment I laid eyes on her. Curse my reckless tongue. Yet even knowing the line I tread is dangerous, I cannot bring myself to take back my bold suggestion.

13

ANYA

I hover awkwardly in the open doorway of my bedroom, watching as Vlad turns down the quilt on the wide bed. Our bed, for tonight at least. The intimate implications of that small word —*our*—make my heart flutter with equal parts anticipation and uncertainty.

"There. It's all ready," Vlad says, grey eyes crinkling with warmth as they meet my timid stare. He gestures invitingly to the turned-down sheets. "Please, make yourself comfortable. I'll sleep atop the covers. Don't worry."

I nod mutely, still hovering on the threshold. Vlad's assured manner helps slow my racing pulse. He intends to stay chivalrous—likely realizing how momentous sharing a bed feels to someone accustomed to solitude, like me. I want to trust his good intentions. My she-wolf certainly does, straining eagerly towards his masculine scent. But old fears have me paralyzed, unable to take that first step over the line.

Sensing my lingering reservations, Vlad moves slowly towards me. He lifts my chin with one rough fingertip, compelling me to meet his earnest stormy gaze.

"You have my word, we will go no further than you wish tonight," he vows solemnly. "Just sleep, nothing more. *You* set the boundaries."

Reassured by his sincerity, I exhale slowly and pad into the room on bare feet. Vlad withdraws to give me space as I slide under the covers he just attentively turned down for me. The sheets still hold his earthy scent, enveloping me in a heady embrace. I ache to pull him down into this nest beside me, wolf and woman stirring as one. But I stay centered on my side, listening to Vlad settle atop the covers beside me after dimming the lamp.

Strangely shy now that we're finally here, I keep my eyes closed and back turned to him. But the awareness of his presence buzzes through me all the same. The mattress sinks slightly under his impressive bulk. I can hear his measured breathing, sense his radiant warmth even with cautious inches still separating us. My frazzled nerves prickle at his proximity, skin flushed as if he's already touching me.

"Goodnight, Anya," Vlad rumbles softly. I nearly jump out of my skin at the sound. His deep timbre so close makes me shiver beneath the covers.

"Goodnight," I whisper back faintly. An expectant hush falls over the room, magnifying each subtle shift and sound. I try to steady my breathing, to find some semblance of my usual composure. But it eludes me, nerves stretched taut as overtuned violin strings.

Turning my mind from the temptation of the man at my side, I focus determinedly on each inhale and exhale. On relaxing every clenched muscle one by one until heaviness seeps into my limbs. I begin drifting at last, despite the circumstances, lulled into drowsiness by rhythmic shared breaths. Vlad's presence feels natural, comforting somehow. My last waking thought is the realization that I haven't felt this safe while sleeping in years...

GRADUALLY, I SURFACE TO MUTED EARLY LIGHT filtering through the curtains. For once, my sleep was not fragmented by restlessness or bleak dreams— only a profound sense of peace lingers. I feel cocooned in warmth, pressed flush against another's body heat.

My eyes fly open, meeting the bare skin of Vlad's shoulder inches from my face. Sometime in the night, we both shifted towards the center of the bed, legs tangling together while his arm cradles me close. His steady heartbeat thuds under my palm splayed on his chest.

I should pull away, rebuild the careful boundaries between us before he wakes. But I cannot make myself break this tender embrace. I want only to nuzzle closer and let Vlad's strength surround me a little longer, his spicy cedar scent lulling me back to contented oblivion.

As if sensing my waking tension, Vlad begins to stir. He inhales deeply, chin nudging the top of my head as his hold tightens reflexively. I feel his lashes flutter against my hair before he pulls back slightly to meet my startled gaze.

Grey eyes widen, surprise and something more primal flashing through them as Vlad takes in our compromising position. I brace for him to retreat, to re-establish careful distance between us. But he just cradles me closer, his calloused thumb tracing delicate shapes on my shoulder.

"Forgive me. I didn't mean to take such liberties,"

Vlad rasps, voice still husky with sleep. His stare drops to my lips and the air suddenly feels electric, charged with possibilities. I wet my dry lips unconsciously. Vlad tracks the movement, leaning infinitesimally nearer...

Abruptly, he seems to recollect himself, releasing me to roll onto his back with a muttered curse. Disappointment pierces through my yearning as inches of cold bedsheet now separate us. I want to reclaim Vlad's warmth, to admit how deeply last night affected me. But vulnerability strangles the reckless words unspoken.

Silence swells uncomfortably. Seeking distraction, I rise briskly and don my robe. "I'll make us some coffee," I murmur without meeting Vlad's eyes. His gaze follows me, heavy as a touch, as I flee the charged room still tingling from our unguarded embrace.

In the kitchen, I try to re-center my scattered emotions. *You're playing with fire,* I scold myself as I light the stove, thoughts churning darker than the brewing coffee. Getting attached to this fascinating stranger will only end in heartbreak when he leaves. I've weathered enough loss in isolation—I mustn't crave more.

I glance out the window as the coffee begins

percolating. Snow heaps in towering drifts, sparkling under the pale predawn light. No sign of it melting anytime soon. We're well and truly snowed in, Vlad and I.

Two mugs in hand, I cautiously re-enter the bedroom. Vlad has risen, raking a hand through his rumpled hair. His toned chest and scarred arms gleam bronze in the pale sunshine, making my pulse skitter. He accepts the coffee with a murmured thanks, fingers grazing mine and igniting sparks once more.

We sip the scalding brew side by side atop the tangled sheets, stealing glances when the other isn't looking. The potent brew helps clear some of the sensual cobwebs from my addled brain. But our shared awakening replays vividly behind my eyes, kindling reckless thoughts of where such dangerous intimacy might lead.

As much as I may yearn to explore this magnetic pull further, I know pursuing it would be utter folly. This interlude out of time will end soon, Vlad returning to his rightful place and me to mine, alone. I would do well to remember that, and not seek more than has already been gifted.

"Let me top you off," Vlad offers, taking the coffee pot to refill our mugs. The domesticity of sharing a morning drink strikes me. He could just as easily have fled to the kitchen, preserving distance. But instead, he lingers, drawn to my company as I am to his.

I tell him about my pressing commissions for Yulia, the progress I'm making on the Saint Petersburg cityscapes so they'll be complete before the roads turn impassable for the season.

Vlad listens attentively, grey eyes focused on me over the curling steam. "Your patron must be very successful to support so many artists," he comments.

I explain Yulia's hotel connections while Vlad asks thoughtful questions, seeming genuinely interested in my humble artistic pursuits. He doesn't brush off my work as mere hobby pieces, as so many do. The realization warms me. Perhaps we connect on levels beyond the obvious physical passion simmering dangerously between us.

When I mention needing to take the finished pieces into town once the snow melts, Vlad sets down his mug decisively. "I'd be happy to accompany you, ensure you get there and back safely. The roads can still be treacherous… As I've learned firsthand." He gestures ruefully to his healing wounds, coaxing a small smile from me.

I hesitate, but sense only sincerity in his offer, not

manipulation. "I'd welcome the company," I say softly.

We share a lingering look of perfect understanding. The moment stretches, more than reasonably. I break it by standing abruptly, pulse racing.

"Well, I should get back to work. Wouldn't want to keep Yulia waiting on her paintings." I force an airy laugh, avoiding his piercing gaze. "I'm afraid life around here is pretty simple and dull. You'll likely get bored."

As I turn to flee, Vlad's firm hand seizes my wrist with an iron grip, halting me in my tracks. "*Nothing* about you or your life is boring to me, Anya." He says it with such stern conviction that a thrill rushes through my veins. My breath hitches as our gazes lock once more, his stormy eyes holding me transfixed.

Mercifully, his grip soon relaxes, allowing me to slip free and regain my scattered composure. Vlad rises smoothly from the bed, restoring careful distance between us.

"Come," he says. "I'll fix us some breakfast before you lose yourself in work. A shower can wait until after."

I just nod mutely, skin still tingling where he grasped me. His sheer determination to care for me even in my own home sets my heart racing dangerously. Steadily, Vlad has begun dismantling my defenses, one fragile brick at a time. Yet I cannot bring myself to shore them back up, to re-enforce the barriers his patient siege threatens to breach.

Not when keeping him near promises such exquisite torment.

14
ANYA

I add the finishing details to the ornate iron lampposts along the snowy Saint Petersburg embankment, heeding Vlad's advice not to become so absorbed in work that I forget basic needs. After being hunched over the easel for hours, my neck and shoulders ache terribly with tension. I rinse my brushes and stand, rolling my stiff joints with a groan. A hot shower might help relax my overtaxed muscles.

Setting my palette aside, I tread quietly down the hall to the bathroom. The mirrors are still hazy with remnants of steam—seems Vlad recently finished his shower. I turn the tap to let the water heat up again, filling the cramped space with fresh billows of steam. The soothing spray will feel heavenly after being stationary, painting all morning.

I'm unbraiding my hair when the pipes begin to groan and knock loudly. "Damn loose couplings," I mutter, making a mental note to ask Vlad to look at them later. Stripping off my paint-specked clothes, I step under the streaming water, moaning in relief as the heat begins penetrating my sore limbs. I stand motionless, letting the tension slowly dissolve from my neck and back.

Abruptly, the pipes give a great shuddering gurgle. Water pressure surges, blasting me in the face. Then the spray cuts out completely with a dying wheeze.

"Oh, no! No, no...!" I gasp, blindly groping for the taps. But it's too late—the ancient water heater has clearly given up the ghost... So much for a soothing shower.

Cursing at the icy drafts now penetrating the steamy bathroom, I grab my towel and start blotting the rivulets from my skin and hair. At least most of the paint and grime rinsed off before the pipes failed. I ring out the sopping mess of my braid as best I can, teeth already chattering. Note to self—chop more firewood for a scalding bath later to make up for this.

I'm struggling to fasten my bra over my still-damp skin when the bathroom door bursts open, letting out a huge cloud of steam to the hallway and bouncing off the adjacent wall with a deafening crack.

With my heart leaping into my throat, I turn to face the intruder, skinny arms raised to protect myself from the attack.

There in the open doorway stands a powerfully built, utterly naked, and dripping-wet Vlad.

We both freeze, eyes locking in mutual mortification. My brain short-circuits taking in every stunning inch of his unclothed body—all hard muscle, still-angry red scars, and smooth golden skin. Rivulets of water track down the deep grooves flanking his abdomen, diverging tantalizingly lower. I can't stop tracing their path, imagination igniting at where they disappear into dark curls surrounding his impressive...

"Shit!" Vlad's startled curse snaps my attention back up at last. His sharp features are nearly purple, eyes saucer-wide. He slaps a broad hand over his groin in belated modesty—he'll need more than that to cover up *that* beast.

"S-sorry Anya," he stammers. "I heard a thud and thought you slipped. I just reacted without thinking."

His face flames even brighter. "I should have called out or something first. I didn't mean to barge in on you like that."

I hold up my hands, signaling wordlessly that further explanation is unnecessary. We remain frozen in a long suspended moment, neither of us able to tear our gazes away, too mesmerized by miles of exposed flesh we know we shouldn't ogle. But gods above, what a magnificent vision he makes.

At last, Vlad seems to revive enough to lunge backward and slam the bathroom door shut between us without another word. The following silence throbs as my heart hammers loudly in my ears. Sweet mercy. Every inch of that chiseled physique is now seared indelibly into my memory. I should be shocked, outraged by his bold intrusion. Instead, burning curiosity wars with my ingrained propriety. Just the glimpse of Vlad bared and vulnerable has left me dizzy with suppressed longing.

The wolf in me whines and claws inside my mind, half-mad from the brief view of our stoic companion stripped of all defenses. She wants to fling that door open again and stare our fill. Wants to trace taut muscle and scar with hands and tongue until we learn all his secret places. My inner minx fully embraces this unexpected chance to devour him with the eyes he usually guards so carefully from prying perception.

Arousal and guilt churn sickeningly in my gut as I gather up my paint-flecked clothes with shaking hands. What on earth has come over me? I need to escape before I do something truly reckless, like begging Vlad to sate these frantic new appetites clawing through my blood.

Yanking a fresh set of garments on with trembling fingers, I stumble from the little cabin, desperate for distance and frigid air to shock some sense back into my addled brain. But even the icy kiss of winter cannot dim the raging fire now lit inside me. There will be no forgetting the magnificent vision of that man bared wholly, his evident desire for me burning hot as my own scarcely-leashed passion.

Whatever happens after this, a single truth remains—the magnetic pull I've tried so hard to deny has only grown stronger between us. And resisting it much longer may prove an impossible feat.

For better or worse, this growing bond transcends propriety or reason now. It runs deeper than flesh and bone. And I cannot stem the tide swelling steadily up from the chambered heart of me, drowning all caution in its swirling flood. The only choice left is whether to fight this relentless current or surrender to its unknown and dangerous depths.

I stand motionless beneath the watchful pines until my skin numbs and my joints ache with cold. But clarity remains elusive. Sighing plumes of mist into the icy air, I turn back towards the humble cabin. However dangerously my balance has shifted today, the path ahead is not mine alone to determine. Vlad's desires hold equal weight, though they remain obscured behind his unreadable facade. I cannot presume to decide for us both based only on my jumbled emotions.

Squaring my shoulders, I slip back inside, bracing for strained awkwardness or defensive distance. But surprisingly, Vlad is composed when I find him at the stove, preparing a simple meal. Aside from lingering color on his sharp cheekbones, his demeanor shows no cracks. Those intent grey eyes meet mine with perfect calm, a hint of humor in their depths.

"There you are," he says lightly. "I was starting to worry you got lost. It's been an hour."

He holds my gaze, daring me to address the elephant in the room. When I make no mention of the earlier incident, something like relief passes over his rugged features. We take refuge in normalcy, carrying on stilted small talk over dinner as if nothing momentous occurred.

Yet the new secret thrums hot between us, binding us in shared forbidden knowledge. As we clear up the meal in awkward silence, my mind races feverishly. How can I possibly share a bed again with Vlad after what happened? After seeing every bare inch of his body that now fuels my restless fantasies?

But neither can I resign him to the unforgiving studio floor after our pact.

I'm contemplating sneaking off to take the floor myself when Vlad's stern voice stops me in my tracks. "Don't even think about it. You're not sleeping on the hard floor tonight."

I open my mouth to protest but he cuts me off. "And neither am I. We share the bed—we agreed that would be best." His eyes soften slightly. "Please. After today's... excitement, we could both use some rest."

His practical words dissolve my protests before they form. Vlad is right, as usual. The reasonable course is sticking to our original agreement. Allowing awkwardness to dictate our actions will only breed more discomfort.

I exhale slowly, releasing some of the anxiety twisting my guts. "You're right. We share." I'm a mature woman. I can handle this… can't I?

The set of Vlad's shoulders relaxes subtly in relief.

We slip under the cool sheets. Side by side in bed, we maintain careful distance. But sleep proves elusive as my awareness of him thrums loudly in the darkness. I lie frozen as if balanced on a precipice, senses attuned to his every breath and rustle. Waiting endlessly for... something.

Until the mattress shifts under Vlad's weight and

warmth envelops me. With exquisite care, he fits our bodies together, legs tangling and arm draping over my tense frame. His stubble grazes my shoulder as his lips find my ear.

"Just sleep, Anya…" he breathes. "I've got you."

My defenses crumble at the tender command. Sheltered in his loose embrace, slumber rises up to claim me at last. Tomorrow's uncertainties seem conquerable wrapped safely in Vlad's strong arms. Tonight, there's only this. And it is enough.

15

VLAD

I awake slowly, senses tuning to the familiar scents and sounds of the cabin. Anya's sweet floral fragrance teases my nose, conjuring memories of the charged moments leading us to share her bed. I had expected restlessness, but slumber claimed me swiftly and deeply despite the novelty of another's warmth nearby.

I open my eyes to pale fading moonlight filtering through the room's small window. Anya lies facing away on the opposite edge of the mattress, dark hair fanned over her pillow. Her breath comes slow and even, still claimed by sleep. Something about watching her unguarded stirs an unexpected protec-tiveness within me. At rest, she seems young, innocent—a vulnerable creature to be shielded from the harsh world.

But I know that perception is only an illusion. Beneath her placid exterior lies a strong spirit, a survivor tested by trials unknown. Anya has a restless wildness too, carefully leashed. I wonder if she dreams of running free, as I often do. Does she feel something similar to me, when my spirited wolf paces relentlessly against the confines of this mundane existence?

What dreams and longings stir beneath those tranquil features? In her waking wariness, I doubt she will allow me to delve deeper anytime soon. But I find myself longing to breach the walls around her heart, to earn passage into her trust. An unaccustomed yearning, for one accustomed to solitude. Yet being near Anya awakens an instinctive protectiveness, a fundamental need to prove myself worthy of her faith.

I startle from my pensive thoughts as Anya stirs and turns to face me. Her eyes flutter open, meeting my intent stare. For a breathless moment she simply gazes back, lips parted softly. Then recollection sweeps over her features and she pulls away, flustered at having been caught off guard.

"Hey, there…" I offer, hoping to set her more at ease.

"Hey," Anya mumbles, sitting up swiftly and putting more distance between us. She avoids looking directly at me now, a pretty blush tinting her defined cheekbones.

Amused, I ask innocently, "Sorry, I woke you. Did you at least sleep well?" I prop myself up against the headboard to appreciate her reaction fully.

Anya's blush deepens. "Well enough," she says shortly. "And… you?"

"Better than I have in some time." I keep my tone light, though the words ring true. Having her comforting presence nearby tempers the bleak thoughts that often haunt my waking mind.

Anya finally meets my eyes again, lips curving into a shy half-smile at my admission. "I'm glad to hear that," she says, voice softening.

Impulsively, I reach out to brush a stray lock of hair from her cheek. Anya's pulse flutters wildly at the brief contact. Emboldened, I let my fingers graze her jaw, captivated by the smooth silk of her skin beneath my rough palm.

"Vlad…" Anya's whisper holds an endearing mix of wanting and uncertainty. I trail my thumb over her parted lips, watching her closely. She does not retreat from my explorations, though her breath comes faster. I take that as permission to continue this intimate study, forging new paths of trust.

With exquisite care, I trace along the graceful slope of Anya's neck, feeling her quickened heartbeat pulsing beneath. She tips her head back instinctively, eyelids sinking closed as she yields to my attentions. Each newly discovered sensitive spot elicits a delightful shiver or hitched breath. I catalog every nuance eagerly, determined to uncover all that will please her.

When my fingers skim lower, grazing her collarbone peeking above her linen shift, Anya's eyes fly open. She seizes my hand, stilling its progress. For a suspended moment, we stare at one other, the growing heat between us near tangible.

"We shouldn't," Anya finally whispers, though she makes no move to break contact.

I entwine our fingers lightly, keeping my touch reverent. "You're right. Forgive me." Anya's safety and dignity are paramount to me, no matter what my reckless instincts may demand. I make to withdraw, but Anya suddenly grips my hand tighter, holding me fast.

"It's alright," she says, eyes drinking in my face as though seeing me clearly for the first time. Her free hand rises tentatively to brush along my bearded jaw. "It's just... I don't give my trust easily."

I turn my head to press a kiss against her delicate palm. "I know. And I am prepared to wait, for however long it takes to earn what you so carefully guard."

Emotion swells in Anya's gaze. No more words are needed. Some doors cannot be rushed or forced, only gently opened when the time is right. Anya gifts me with a smile that sets my pulse racing anew. But there is a solemnity in her expression now too, an unspoken understanding passing between us. From this point on, nothing will be the same.

As Anya's fingertips graze my lips with excruciating tenderness, the atmosphere hangs heavy with promise. But I know all possibilities must wait for her, left to blossom further. Patience has never been my strength; yet for her, I will temper the wildness in my blood however needed.

When Anya finally withdraws her hand, the loss leaves me bereft. Yet her shy parting caress awakens hope as well. She does not reject this dangerous fascination growing between us—she merely slows its pace for both our sakes. Wise, compassionate Anya. In her capable hands, perhaps even one as battered and burdened as I may find healing...

Suddenly, she leans in and presses her petal-soft lips to mine in a gentle kiss. I freeze, stunned by her bold initiation. But soon, instinct takes over and I return the kiss reverently, letting Anya set the pace.

Her mouth moves slowly against my own, sending sparks arcing through my entire body. The kiss remains relatively chaste, but conveys a well of longing. When we finally part, Anya looks slightly embarrassed by her own audacity.

"Was that alright?" she asks in a whisper.

I brush my thumb over her kiss-swollen lower lip, desire coursing wildly through me. "It was perfect."

Anya's expression morphs into pure joy. She kisses me again, more firmly this time. My heart soars at this new level of trust and intimacy we've attained. I've never felt such a profound connection to another soul. Her name becomes a prayer upon my lips as we lose ourselves in this unhurried exploration of each other.

Every touch, every stolen breath, seems to deepen the bond between us. Anya's hands find their way into my hair, her fingers tangling in the strands as she pulls me closer. Our bodies melt together, a perfect fit, as if we were made for each other. Time loses all meaning as we traverse this uncharted territory of desire and vulnerability.

In one painful moment, Anya breaks the kiss, her chest rising and falling with an intoxicating mix of anticipation and uncertainty. Her eyes search mine for reassurance, seeking confirmation that what we're embarking on is real and true.

I caress her cheek, my thumb tracing the curve of her jawline. "Anya," I whisper, my voice filled with a newfound tenderness. "We don't have to rush this. We have all the time in the world."

It's a big step for her, and I refuse to push any harder. My inner wolf may be growling in protest, but I quell him with ease. It becomes clear to me then— nothing will ever take precedence over my beloved Anya.

Her voice shudders when she says, "I can't fight this any longer, Vlad... I won't." She gazes at me, smoldering brown eyes burning into mine. "I need you."

I glide a firm hand along her soft jawline. "Are you sure?"

Her eyes darken with determination as she nods, her breath coming in ragged gasps. "Yes," she whispers, her voice filled with a mix of desire and vulnerability.

My heart pounds in my chest, overwhelmed by the weight of her words.

Anya's breath quickens as I lower my lips to hers once more. The world outside these four walls fades into insignificance as we find ourselves entangled in a dance of desire and trust. Her soft moans fill the space, mingling with mine, drawing us deeper into the realm of passion and surrender.

16

ANYA

As Vlad's lips meet mine again, a tempest of emotions whirls within me. His kiss, so full of intent and promise, makes the walls I have meticulously built around my heart tremble. Each gentle tug, each soft moan that escapes from the depths of my throat feels like a crack in my armor, a sweet unraveling of years of solitude and flight.

My hands, once tools of survival, now tangle in his hair, pulling him closer as if he were a lifeline. The rough texture of his locks between my fingers grounds me to the moment, to the undeniable reality of Vlad's presence. The warmth of our bodies melding together defies the coldness I have known for too long.

As our kiss deepens, the rogue in me—the wild, the untamed—whispers caution. But the wolf in me, the one aching for connection, silences her with a desperate hunger. Vlad's touch ignites a fire that no sense of duty or fear will ever extinguish. His reverence in every caress speaks to a part of me I hadn't realized was pleading to be acknowledged, to be cherished.

"Oh, gods... Anya... You undo me," he murmurs, voice resonating with lustful frankness.

My heart clenches at his naked admission. I draw him back to me, pouring all my jumbled emotions into another searing kiss, unable to verbalize a reply. I hope my touch can convey what words cannot—that Vlad has awakened something in me too. Something frightening and exhilarating. That the thought of losing this fragile connection terrifies me to my core.

But I can't think of that now. I force myself not to linger on the painful moments of my past, or the reason why I'm running from the pack. I want only to be present in this moment, to be his—no matter what the future may bring. If there is pain ahead, then so be it. That's a price I'm willing to pay for this sweet taste of bliss.

Lazily, we strip from our clothes, the fabric falling to the floor in a heap, as we continue to explore each other's bodies with an unspoken hunger. His firm hands trace the curves of my waist, leaving trails of fire in their wake. I surrender to the sensation, allowing myself to be consumed by the intensity of our connection.

The cool sheets embrace us as we fall onto the bed, limbs entwined and hearts pounding. Naked and unashamed, Vlad's eyes roam over my body with a hunger that mirrors my own.

Vlad's lips trail down my neck, his tongue flicking over my heated skin, sending shivers down my spine. His hands, strong and sure, claim the curve of my hips, guiding me closer to him. It's then that I feel it —the hardness of his arousal pressing against me, demanding as it seeks entrance. With a moan, I lift my hips invitingly, silently begging for more.

He obliges, sliding into me inch by tantalizing inch. His girth fills me completely, stretching me in ways I had long forgotten or perhaps only ever dreamed of. The heat of his invasion sears through my veins, igniting a fire I thought long extinguished. It feels so right—so very right—to be joined with him in this primal way.

As he begins to move within me, our hips slapping together in an untamed rhythm that echoes through the room, I arch my back and revel in the delicious friction. My nails dig into his back, scorching his skin as I urge him onward, upward, craving more of this connection that transcends all reason.

The pleasure intensifies tenfold when he brushes against a spot within me that no other lover has ever found—a place that sets my world ablaze and has me gasping his name like a fervent prayer. Vlad growls low in response, his thrusts becoming even more frantic, more animalistic as his desire for me spirals out of control. Heat pools deep within me, coiling tighter and tighter, ready to explode like a comet in the night sky.

With one last thrust, he presses deeper than before, and I gasp in ecstasy, my senses overwhelmed by the fullness of him within me. My inner walls clench around him like a vice, desperate to keep him inside me forever. It takes everything I have not to shatter into a million pieces right then and there.

"Yes," I moan. "Yes!" The edge of ecstasy is so close I can taste it. "Don't stop."

"Don't move," he grunts out in response, his voice rough with arousal as he slows his pace, his hips suddenly still. His body trembles above mine, every muscle taut with restraint as he struggles for control.

"But, I can't..." I pant, the pleasure so close, but just out of reach. "I have to... Vlad, I *need* to come."

He growls low in response, his shoulders

bunching with effort. He mutters a curse. "I should've used protection…"

It then dawns on me—the maddening pressure, the overwhelming fullness of him. He's *knot-deep* inside me. But then, that would mean… Oh, gods. He's a wolf shifter. *Vlad is a fucking wolf shifter.*

"It's alright," I mumble, remaining as still as I can, which is almost impossible with this gorgeous man on top of me. "I'm not in heat."

He startles, stormy eyes wide as they fix on mine. "Wait a minute," he stammers. "You're a wolf too?"

I nod, feeling vulnerable and exposed. Well, it's finally out there. What is he going to do now?

Vlad's eyes bore into mine, and I see the storm of emotions raging within them: shock, disbelief, and… desire. His grip on my hips tightens as he draws back only to thrust deep within me once more, causing me to cry out in pleasure.

"Then, you know what this means. Don't you?" he growls, his voice low and husky.

"What?" I manage to breathlessly ask, my brain swimming with lust and the overwhelming sensation between my legs.

"We're mates," he whispers in my ear, his warm breath sending shivers down my spine. In that moment, everything clicks into place. The undeniable pull I felt towards him. The unspent longing that plagued me for months. It all makes sense now. He's the one I have been waiting for all along—*my other half.*

His words send a supernova of pleasure through me as the weight of our connection finally sinks in. My climax crashes over me like a tidal wave, and I scream out in ecstasy, white-hot lightning coursing through every nerve ending as the world dissolves around us. Vlad follows suit, his entire body tensing as he finds his release inside me.

While our bodies move together in the throes of passion, Vlad's cock twitches within me in a way that speaks of possession and ownership. The thought should be terrifying, but instead, it only stokes the flames of my desire. *He's my mate. My fated match.* The one I've been destined for all my life. The realization is both thrilling and terrifying. But right now, all I can focus on is the delicious friction between us.

As my orgasm subsides, I feel Vlad's knot swell inside me, locking us together. I bite my lip to muffle a moan, the sensation oddly arousing and comforting at the same time. He collapses onto me, his chest heaving with each ragged breath as we both gasp for air. His eyes glow silver with a mixture of desire, lust, and something else—can it be love? Gods, it's too soon for that... right?

"Vlad," I whisper through trembling lips, tears prickling beneath my eyelids. "I... I don't know what to say."

He sweeps me in his arms, holding me tight. "No need for words," he pants. "We'll figure this out." A heavy sigh of contentment escapes him.

Suddenly, he flinches as if finally realizing something. "Hold up," he grunts. "Where's your brand?" His gaze darts around my body frantically, searching for the pack emblem that should be inked on my skin. "I don't see one on you…"

"I don't... have one," I confess. "I'm a rogue." The words bring back painful memories, so I leave it at that. Just then, the slightest shift of his hips reignites the flames of my desire. Gods, I'm so full of him. So close to the edge once more.

"Oh... fuck…" he growls, gritting his teeth. Was that a cry of worry or pleasure? I can't tell. But whatever it was, it only increased my craving for him.

"This is so messed up," Vlad mutters, sweeping a hand across his brow.

"Yeah…" I murmur low, suddenly feeling too self-conscious and unworthy. I'm a packless wolf, a rogue living in exile. He deserves better than me.

But then Vlad pulls me closer, his voice husky with desire. "And *I want to keep* messing it up," he purrs, sending shivers down my spine. "D'you want that?" Without waiting for my answer, he seals my mouth with his in a series of deep sultry kisses that make my toes curl.

"Uh-huh…" I manage in a quiet moan the second our lips part briefly.

Vlad grins wickedly as he begins trailing kisses down my neck, his fingers dancing along my body, igniting little fires in their wake. It's as if the consummation of our mating bond has only fanned the flames of our desire for each other. He then glides on top of me, his body pressing me into the plush mattress, and renews his kisses with a newfound hunger. His length, still hard and intrusive inside me, begins to swell again, growing even harder within my walls. I run my fingers through his dark locks, moaning as he teases my sensitive spots, and I arch my hips towards him, craving more contact.

Vlad growls in response to my eagerness, his canines lengthening involuntarily. "Goddess, you're irresistible," he groans before claiming my lips in a deep kiss, thrusting his tongue into my mouth in tandem with his hips rocking against mine. The sensation sends shivers down my spine and I wrap my legs around his waist, urging him on as he starts moving within me in a slow yet relentless rhythm.

His pace steadily increases, driving us both higher and higher until we're panting for air. His thrusts become more intense and erratic, and I know that he's close to the edge again. I arch my back to meet him stroke for stroke, panting desperately as wave after wave of pleasure washes over me. Heat flares in my core, coiling tighter and tighter, begging for release. Vlad's growls of pleasure fill the room, spurring me on to match his primal moans.

As we both reach the peak of delight, our bodies shuddering together in bliss, I feel something warm and viscous pulsing deep inside me, sealing our bond. The unfamiliar sensation only heightens my orgasm, and I dig my nails into his back as I clench around him.

"Mine," he growls, his breath hot in my ear. "You're mine now, Anya… forever."

Vlad's thrusts slow down and eventually stop as we both catch our breaths, our chests heaving.

"Holy… fuck," he pants, collapsing on top of me, his length still inside me. "That… was… unreal."

I manage a breathless laugh, my chest rising and falling rapidly. "Tell me about it."

We stay like that for what feels like hours, basking in the afterglow of our shared release.

Slowly, our breathing returns to normal, and the world around us comes back into focus. Outside the window, sunrise kisses the horizon, filling the room with a golden haze. But neither of us seems to care about time or the outside world at this moment. All that matters is each other's warmth and this newfound connection between us.

I've found him. At last. My soul is complete.

17

ANYA

I slowly drift awake, silken sheets pooled around my bare skin. Pale golden light filters through the curtains, announcing the evening's approach. For a long moment, I simply bask limply in the cozy nest of blankets, deliciously sore in all the right places.

As waking thoughts begin to take shape, memory comes flooding back in a dizzying rush—the passion shared, the electric bliss of our joined bodies, and afterwards, the breathtaking realization that Vlad is my mate. *Mine.* The enormity of it sends a heady thrill through me even now.

Eager to see him again, I reach across the rumpled linens seeking Vlad's solid warmth. But my roving hand finds only empty space where he should lay.

Disappointment pierces through the haze of waking at his absence. Until I hear the shower start up in the adjoining bathroom, realization dawning—Vlad readying himself for the evening ahead.

I stretch lazily, skin tingling with recollected sensations from our intense lovemaking. Nestled here surrounded by Vlad's earthy scent, it seems impossible that after so many cold, lonely seasons barely surviving as a lone wolf, I could discover such perfect belonging in another's arms.

Yet somehow, fate saw fit to deliver this man unto me, two kindred souls finding solace together. A gift I silently vow never to take for granted, no matter the trials still ahead. For once in my weary existence, the future feels bright with hope.

The bathroom door creaks open, trailing wisps of fragrant steam into the bedroom. Vlad's imposing silhouette fills the doorway, black hair dripping rivulets down his flushed bare chest. He halts when he notices I'm awake, stormy grey eyes softening as they meet my own.

"There's my sleepy beauty," he rumbles fondly. Beads of water still cling to his heated skin, a damp towel wrapped loosely around his lean hips. I drag my gaze hungrily over all that exposed muscle and tanned flesh, mouth going dry. Vlad notices my staring and smirks, clearly enjoying the effect his stunning physique has on me.

"See something you like?" he asks with faux innocence, flexing subtly so light plays over the grooves flanking his abdomen.

I roll my eyes, flinging a pillow at him. Vlad dodges it easily, chuckling. "Get dressed, you insufferable man," I scold without heat.

Vlad's grin only widens at my flustered reaction before he turns to oblige. I allow myself a moment to admire his sculpted back appreciatively before it disappears beneath a shirt.

Once presentably attired in borrowed clothes, Vlad perches on the edge of the rumpled bed and draws me close. His expression shifts to something more serious and searching.

"How are you feeling?" He cups my cheek, rough thumb stroking over my skin tenderly. "After everything that's happened between us?"

I understand his meaning. He refers not just to the wonderful intimacy we shared, but the profound emotional impact of finding one's fated mate. I cover Vlad's broad hand with my own, warmth blooming in my chest under his concern. "I'm… wonderful," I assure him sincerely. And it's true—despite my lingering anxieties about the future, in this moment I've never felt more safe, cherished, or complete.

Visible relief and suppressed emotion shine in Vlad's stormy eyes. He swallows thickly before trust seems to win out over his masculine reservations.

"Good. I admit, I still can hardly believe your wolf called to mine so strongly," he says roughly. Clearing his throat, Vlad stands and draws me up too, keeping our hands entwined. "I made us dinner. But first, we should talk."

My pulse kicks faster at those ominous words. I'm unaccustomed to letting anyone in or speaking of the painful history that forced me to live in seclusion. But Vlad and I are bound now—it's only fair I bare my damaged soul to him too in return for the gift of his body and trust.

Sensing my building anxiety, Vlad squeezes my hand soothingly and leads us downstairs to the cozy kitchen. I brace myself for the interrogation about my past, but instead, Vlad begins hesitantly relating his own tale first.

"You deserve to know who I really am and how I came to be here," he starts haltingly.

Vlad shares openly, for the first time ever, about his beginnings as the runt of his pack, abandoned at birth and taken in by the powerful Alpha of a bear shifter clan.

He then speaks of the vicious fight with his treacherous kin Grisha, defending his brother's mate only to catastrophically fail in his familial duty. The painful loss of his former life and pack bonds when he was left behind, bloody and dying, haunts Vlad still.

He speaks candidly of feeling adrift and ashamed, a guardian who could not safeguard those who mattered most—his only remaining family. I listen in compassionate silence, cradling Vlad's shaking scarred hands in mine in wordless support. This honed fighter prides strength and control, but exposing these still-raw wounds makes him vulnerable, almost childlike.

"I don't even know if my brother still lives," Vlad finishes bleakly. "But I fear Grisha yet draws breath, and if so, he remains a threat. You must be wary, my Anya." His stare blazes with conviction as he grips my shoulders. "I vow to you here and now, I will not fail in protecting you or our future together. Never again."

My heart clenches, moved by this proud wolf's determination to defend me, even after all he has suffered. When Vlad finally falls quiet, drained by the emotional confession, I pull him into a fierce embrace. He stiffens briefly, before relaxing into my arms with a shuddering exhale.

"What happened to your family was not your fault," I whisper fiercely against his raven hair. "But now, the bond between us is ours to build, unburdened by the past."

It becomes clear to me now. Vlad carries the heavy mantle of being the beta son, in the shadow of his Alpha brother Gavriil's legacy. But in my eyes, none of those roles and burdens matter. He doesn't need to prove anything. He just needs to be himself.

Vlad shudders against me, some of the rigid tension leaving his powerful frame at my absolution. I ache to permanently erase the survivor's guilt and grief still haunting this fighter, to soothe unseen scars as our bodies learned to do last night. For now, freely offering my acceptance is all I can give. But I sense it's enough.

Eventually, Vlad draws back, eyes glimmering with emotion though his overall expression seems lighter than before. He gifted me his darkest demons —it seems only fair I now offer mine in return, to complete this baring of souls. But as I open my mouth hesitantly, Vlad presses a finger to my lips, stilling the painful words.

"You don't have to reveal your past until you're ready," he says gently. "I can and *will* wait patiently for as long as it takes, until fate chooses the right time for you to unburden yourself."

Profound relief and gratitude sweep through me, loosening the anxious knot in my gut. After so long bottling up the trauma of my escape, the fact that Vlad does not demand or expect me to pour it all out immediately just to satisfy some notion of parity is the most precious gift.

Unable to articulate my swirling emotions, I simply pull his handsome face down to mine for a kiss imbued with all the things caught in my throat. Vlad smiles against my lips, hands coming up to cradle my jaw tenderly as we lose ourselves for a blissful moment.

When we finally drift apart, his forehead rests against mine as we breathe each other's air, everything outside this bubble fading away to insignificance. All that matters now is us—this man who has come to mean everything to me in such a short time, and who miraculously seems to feel the same. However uncertain and perilous the future, we will face it united. And that knowledge alone settles my shaken soul.

Vlad caresses my cheek reverently, thumb tracing over the markings he left there last night when passion overruled gentleness. "Come now. You must be starving," he says gruffly, pulling us both to our feet. We make our way to the pantry, wounds old and new soothed simply by our continued shared closeness.

Tomorrow, I will pick up my neglected brush and capture the vivid winter landscape outside our window that has been my longstanding inspiration. And when the time comes, I will slowly unravel the shrouded fibers of my history for Vlad too. But for now, I am content simply to stand at this extraordinary man's side, all the lonely gaps inside me filled by his presence.

18

ANYA

A full moon hangs heavy in the star-strewn sky as I slip from the warm shelter of our bed, leaving Vlad sleeping peacefully under the covers. The cabin air chills my bare skin as I dress silently, but anticipation warms me from within.

Tonight, I'm drawn outside by the moon's irresistible call, longing to shed my human form and revel purely in my wolfskin again. Ever since Vlad branded and claimed me as his fated mate, my inner creature stirs franticly, glorying in our completed bond. Under the moon's glow, I can answer that primal urge to run wild and free.

I make my way down the snowy path away from the cabin, senses heightened. The wind gusts bitter against my cheeks, but I revel in its cold bite. The chill focuses me, gives me purpose. I walk for some time under the silent sentinels of the pines, letting their solemn strength realign my scattered thoughts.

I halt at the edge of the tree line, lifting my face to the moon's hypnotic glow. Out here, away from Vlad and the heady spell of his presence, I can think clearly again. Yet even now, my traitorous heart whispers that I should turn back, take refuge in the shelter of his arms...

No. With an effort, I force my feet onward into the shadowed forest. What Vlad and I both need is some space and time alone under our mistress moon's cool light. Time to remember ourselves, and why anything more between us can only lead to ruin when this snowbound dream ends.

The gods have cursed us with an unbreakable bond that defies all logic and reason. He is a wild, untamable creature, destined to wander freely while I am condemned to a life of constant fleeing. The demons from my past claw at my mind relentlessly, threatening to consume me. And yet, I persist in revealing my darkest secrets to Vlad, risking his rejection—a risk that tears at my heart, but one I must take for a chance at true love.

At last, I come to my favorite overlook, a snow-blanketed outcropping of rock jutting over the vast lake below. I settle atop the frigid stone, peering down at the ice gleaming silver under the moon. Solitude enfolds me in its comforting mantle once more.

I close my eyes, releasing the doubts and longings that cling so tenaciously back at the cabin. Out here, I need be nothing more than the wild creature who has always lived inside me, lurking beneath the facade I show the world. With Vlad, I want to be that hidden part of myself again—to run reckless and free, answerable only to the moon. But it cannot be.

Making my decision, I stand swiftly and begin shedding garments. Naked now, I tip back my head with eyes closed... and let go. Bones pop and stretch. Fur ripples up my limbs as four feet settle beneath me. The chill air caresses my wolfskin as I slowly open my eyes again. The world seems simpler through a wolf's gaze.

I turn north, drawn by icy glitter. Padding up to the cliff's edge, I gaze down at the moon's reflection fracturing the frozen lake below. Its beauty pierces me with a familiar longing. Often, I've sat here, muzzle lifted in a mournful howl, serenading the lunar face I sense recognizes me even when no one else does. My confidante, my compass when lost.

Tonight, the urge rises again to sing to the moon my devotion. I fill my lungs, prepared to let loose the threads of my aching heart—when a resounding howl shatters the silence first. My voice dies in my throat.

I whirl, a snarl rumbling warningly—and freeze at the sight before me. A massive black wolf watches from the tree line, silver eyes lambent with lunar light. *Vlad.* Of course, he would feel the pull too, and follow my trail here.

Fur bristling warily, I stand immobilized by indecision. Vlad makes no move to approach, merely continues studying me with an inscrutable intensity that sees down to my soul. I should flee... but my paws root to the spot, caught in his burning stare.

Finally, Vlad stirs, dropping his head submissively. Still telegraphing no aggression, he creeps forward one careful step at a time. I hold tense, trembling with the urge to run for the sanctuary of the woods. But I cannot retreat from this encounter now that we have seen each other plainly at last.

Vlad's rumbling whine shivers through me when only a few paces separate us. He circles, allowing me to take in the full magnificence of his wolf—thick obsidian fur rippling over powerful muscle, deadly fangs peeking past his lips. My white coat would appear diminutive and frail beside his imposing bulk.

Yet I sense no menace in the cautious way he carries himself. Only respect tinged by wonder colors his earthy scent. Still, I flinch when the cold tip of his nose brushes my shoulder in greeting.

At my skittish reaction, Vlad immediately withdraws, a small wounded noise escaping him. Shame flares within me. I should not fear the one who has shown me nothing but selfless kindness since I dragged his broken body in from the cold.

Steeling myself, I stretch out my neck tentatively and bump my muzzle against his in reciprocation. Vlad's answering rumble vibrates through me, even as his body sags in relief.

We remain that way for some time, snuffling and familiarizing ourselves with each other's lupine forms. My initial wariness fades, replaced by comfort in his steadfast presence. After so long bereft of companionship outside my own, discovering such easy acceptance is a balm to my guarded soul. For the first time since that night I found Vlad bloodied and unconscious in the snow, I feel wholly known. And still cared for.

I turn away, moving to the cliff's edge overlooking the moonlit lake. Vlad hangs back respectfully until I glance over my shoulder and chuff in invitation. He settles beside me, so close our bodies press together for shared warmth. The intimacy no longer frightens me as it once did. We were meant to keep each other from the cold.

Together, we serenade the watching moon, our entwined voices soaring in glad chorus to the stars. I have not felt such joy since I was a young pup still surrounded by my pack, free from heartache or betrayal. This one perfect moment with Vlad feels like coming home.

I know not what the new dawn will bring when we awake as man and woman again. But under our lady moon's glow, only this matters—the comfort of skin and fur pressed close, the harmony of our spirit voices uniting in the wilderness that raised us both. Here, now, we are kindred, and the rest can wait.

Eventually, we leave the moon's majesty behind and lope side by side back through the silent woods. But the easy accord forged between us lingers on. I shall carry it like a talisman against darker days ahead when Vlad and I must part ways at long last. Even then, I will cherish knowing that for a fleeting while beneath the winter moon, we were two creatures remade whole together. And no power of this earth can diminish such memories.

19

ANYA

The biting wind howls outside the frosted windowpanes as I add the finishing touches to my latest landscape. Soft bristles glide over the textured canvas, bringing to life the vivid scene before me—snow-coated firs leaning heavily under the burden of ice, their branches etched in silvers and blues gleaming in the pale dawn light. This is the last piece I need to complete Yulia's commission. It won't take long for me to apply my signature in the bottom right corner. The collection will be ready then for installation in her latest hotel project.

I step back, rolling the tension from my shoulders. My empty mug sits cold on the work table, remnants of chamomile tea leaves stuck to the bottom. The clock on the wall reads half past ten. I must have lost track of time again, absorbed in capturing every nuance of the wintry landscape.

I'm wondering where Vlad is. I haven't seen him since breakfast when he shoveled down eggs and sausage in hearty bites before heading out to chop firewood. His healing has improved so much lately that he relishes the opportunity to tackle hands-on projects and repairs. Over the past week, I've heard the echoes of hammering and sawing, interspersed with Russian and Italian curses when something puts up a stubborn fight. But Vlad is nothing if not tenacious.

I smile thinking of his grin when he presented me with a simple wooden tray for my art supplies, etched with an ornate A. His hands are so strong, but can be incredibly gentle. *Gentle...* the smile slips from my face as a wave of dizziness hits me. I grip the back of my chair for balance. What is that about? Probably nothing. Just fatigue and the fumes catching up with me after being cooped up painting with oils all morning. I definitely should have cracked that window wider for better ventilation. The odor of the solvent I used to clean my brushes didn't seem so potent, though.

A deep, longing exhale escapes my lips as I step

into the bathroom. A nice shower is in order to refresh myself.

Turning the brass handles, I release a gush of hot water that sends curls of steam swirling up to the ceiling.

Soon, I am stepping blissfully into the water's enveloping warmth, the heat seeping into my weary muscles. But as I relax, eyes closed, a nagging ache blooms low in my belly. I shift, trying to get comfortable, but the discomfort only grows.

Regrettably, the water cools and I reluctantly step out, skin flushed pink. After toweling off, I choose a soft cream sweater and linen pants from the antique wardrobe. As I braid back my damp hair, an unsettling realization creeps over me. These strange sensations... they remind me of my youth, when my first heat caught me unaware.

No. It can't be. I shake my head sharply, as if I could physically dislodge the notion. I don't have heats anymore. Not since I left the pack. A rogue omega like me is broken, defective. This is surely just exhaustion, or maybe catching a cold after being out sketching in the freezing dawn mornings.

Ignoring the growing ache, I head to the kitchen to make lunch. One look in the antique icebox confirms Vlad hasn't been exaggerating this morning about running low on supplies. With all the projects he's immersed in, I know going to town for groceries would likely fall to me. If the roads were clear, I would enjoy the chance to wander into the quaint shops. But even the thought of venturing so far from the warmth and comfort of our little cabin right now makes my stomach clench anxiously.

I nibble half-heartedly on slices of brown bread spread with the last of the butter, almost gagging as the fatty richness hits my tongue. My inner wolf cringes away from the cloying taste. Suddenly, even the thought of cooking something more substantial is unbearable.

Resigned, I return to my studio to tidy up in preparation for delivering the finished pieces to Yulia. As I straighten my supplies, I fan myself with a sheet of drawing paper. An unnatural heat suffuses my skin, radiating in waves that leave me short of breath. I lean my burning forehead against the soothing chill of the broad windowpane. Snowflakes drift lazily down, the peaceful sight at odds with my inner turmoil.

What is happening to me? I shuffle back to my room, each step weighted with reluctance. But I can't hide here forever. When Vlad returns, he will take one look at me and know.

The thought sends a bolt of fear straight to my

core. I can't let him see me like this. Vulnerable. Needing. Broken.

An escape presents itself in the pile of Vlad's clothes, ready to be laundered. I quickly sort through them, searching for a shirt he wouldn't miss. My fingers settle on a grey cotton Henley, the soft material carrying his earthy, masculine scent. Gripping the shirt like a life preserver, I retreat to my studio and bury myself in the nest I've crafted from Vlad's bedding. His stalwart aroma envelops me, soothing my ragged nerves. I hunker down, clutching one of his pillows as tremors rack my frame. Maybe if I just stay here, ride it out alone, he will be none the wiser when this strange fever breaks...

I must have dozed off, because suddenly Vlad's voice is calling my name. I jolt awake, disoriented. How long have I been tucked away in here?

20

VLAD

The echo of my boots reverberates through the stone corridors as I make my way to Anya's workroom, a tray of roasted chicken and vegetables balanced in one hand. My breath comes out in impatient huffs. As my wounds finally begin to close, I must shift my focus to the upcoming hunt for Grisha. However, Anya has been strangely absent all day, lost in her art within the confines of her studio. I've been mindful not to distract her from work, but she's skipped meals altogether. I won't have her neglecting her self-care this way.

I rap sharply on the door. "I brought you dinner," I call out gruffly.

"I'm not hungry, thanks..." Her muffled voice

sounds small and strained, immediately putting me on alert.

I turn the ornate handle and let myself in, the heavy oak door creaking open. The room is dim, illuminated only by the first beams of moonlight straying through the window. My eyes adjust quickly, zeroing in on the petite form bundled tightly in blankets in the studio's corner.

For a second, I panic, wondering why she would consider returning to our old sleeping arrangements. Has she grown tired of my presence? My mind whirls with endless worries until I pick up the scent that permeates the room—*my* scent on the covers that surround her.

"You need to eat, Anya," I insist, setting the tray down on the work table with a thud.

"I don't want to." She refuses to look at me, burrowing deeper into her den of covers.

I cross my arms. "Is everything alright?"

"Yeah," she murmurs. "I'm just… tired."

I crouch down and grasp her chin, forcing her to meet my piercing gaze. Her skin feels overly warm. "I don't think that's it…" I hesitate to say more, but finally, I spill it. "My heart, I think you're in heat."

Pink blooms on her pale cheeks as she knocks my hand away in embarrassment. "What? No, I'm not!"

I take in her hooded eyes, fatigue evident in every feature of her lovely face. She's being stubborn, but I know the signs.

"Oh... I see," I murmur, then toe off my boots and join her on the plush makeshift bed. She recoils slightly as I wrap my powerful arms around her.

"Shh. I know what you need..." I whisper, enveloping her slender frame with my much larger one. I stroke her chestnut hair and let out a deep rumble from my chest to soothe her. Gradually, the tension eases from her body and she curls into me with a contented sigh, comforted by her Alpha's reassuring presence.

"Is that better, now?" I purr as she buries her face in my chest.

She nods in silence.

We lay entwined as darkness falls, the rhythmic sound of my heartbeat and the warmth of my body giving her shelter from the storm of heat-fever wracking her entire being.

Evening slowly darkens the room. I will stay for as long as she needs, protecting my mate in her vulnerable state. All else can wait.

"Vlad?" she suddenly says.

"Mmm," I growl, possessively encircling her slender waist and pulling her towards me. A smirk tugs at my lips as her supple curves mold against my hard body, perfectly fitting like puzzle pieces.

"Vlad..." she purrs, her voice dripping with desire as she moves her hips against me, seeking out the hardness that has grown between my legs. "I need you."

I close my eyes, fighting the urge to groan as arousal surges through my veins. I know this is a classic side effect of a shifter's heat. But still, it takes all my willpower to resist her. "Anya," I purr. "You know this isn't right. It's the fever talking."

She shrugs off my protests, her hands trailing along the ridges of my abdomen, nails leaving tingling trails in their wake. "I don't care *what* it is. I need you, now." Her hips roll again, more insistent this time.

I growl low in my throat, my restraint close to breaking. The scent of her arousal fills the air, maddening me. "Anya, please... you're in heat... you don't want this."

"Yes. I do," she whimpers, pressing herself against me even tighter. "I've never wanted anything more." She moans as she licks her lips seductively.

Her sweet scent engulfs me like a wave, and I curse under my breath as my resolve crumbles like sand under a raging river. She's irresistible like this—eager and uninhibited, her eyes clouded with need. She raises her hips ever so slightly, grinding against my rigid arousal, a silent demand that I cannot deny her.

"Alright," I grumble, "but just this once."

Anya's answering groan is drowned out by my fervent kisses as I crush her soft lips beneath mine. Her sweet, intoxicating scent fills my nostrils, making me dizzy with need. With a growl of hunger, I peel away each layer of her clothing, revealing her naked form bathed in the moonlight streaming through the window. Her skin is like cream, luminous and smooth to the touch. My mouth trails a line of fire down her neck, pausing to nip on the point where her life force pulses wildly. She whimpers, arching her back, inviting more contact.

I oblige, my hands roaming over every inch of her body as if it's my last chance. Her full breasts spill into my palms, hardened nipples aching for attention. I lavish them with rough kisses, sucking and teasing until she moans for more. Lower still, I let my hands explore the damp heat between her thighs. Her scent is intoxicating—a heady mix of arousal and womanhood that makes my wolf howl in approval. She moans and writhes under my skilled touch, her legs trembling as I tease the swollen folds of the place of her pleasure. Her nectar coats my fingers, and I can't resist a taste. I delve my tongue inside her, eliciting a long moan from her lips.

"Vlad," she moans my name like a prayer, "I've never... felt... this way before."

I smirk against her core, loving the power I have over her sensitized body. My fingers and tongue explore her depths, finding every sensitive spot that makes her shudder and moan. She's so wet, so ready for me. I know she's lost to sheer rapture when she digs her nails into the covers, mindless with need.

"That good?" I ask, every inch the smug Alpha as I lazily circle her swollen bud. "You like how it feels?"

"Yes," she pants, rocking her hips against my face. "More... *please*... more."

I snicker darkly before straightening and taking in the sight before me: Anya, flushed and breathless, her chest heaving with each ragged breath. Her eyes meet mine, pupils dilated with lust and another emotion I dare not name. Before she can protest, I scoop her up in my arms and take her to the bedroom.

I lay her on the bed. Her legs fall open invitingly, revealing the slick folds that beg for attention. I position myself at her entrance, my rock-hard length throbbing against her heat.

"Are you sure about this, Anya?" I growl, fighting the primal urge to plunge inside her depths. "Once we cross this line, there's no going back."

Her response is a hungry moan as she raises her hips in invitation, silky folds parting to welcome me in. With a growl of surrender, I plunge into her wet embrace, and a torrent of sensations floods my senses. She's hot, wet, and so tight around me. Her inner muscles grip me like a vice, ratcheting up the pleasure tenfold.

Anya's nails dig into my skin as she arches her back, taking more of me inside her. I move slowly at first, easing us both into a rhythm that soon turns frantic. Her moans spur me on, each desperate sound driving me deeper into her abyss. I want to claim every inch of her, brand her as mine and mine alone.

"Vlad!" she cries out in a breathy moan as I hit an especially sensitive spot deep within her. "Oh, Goddess! Right there!"

I grin smugly as I continue to hit that spot with every thrust, eliciting more pleasured moans from those beautiful lips. Sweat glistens on our bodies, and the scent of their mingled arousal fills the air, intoxicating and primal. Anya's nails rake down my back, urging me on as her body arches off the sheets, seeking more of my hardness.

"Oh, yes!" she moans, her voice a wanton cry that sends a shiver down my spine. I growl in response, lost in the heady haze of lust and need. My grip on her hips tightens as I thrust harder, driving us both to the brink of ecstasy. Her inner muscles clench around me, milking my length with mind-numbing pressure.

"So tight," I grunt between clenched teeth. "You feel so damn good, Anya." My eyes lock with hers, two beings caught up in the throes of unadulterated passion.

Her legs wrap around my waist, ankles crossed behind my back, pulling me even closer as she tips her head back with a cry. Her breasts bounce enticingly with every powerful thrust, and I can't help but marvel at the sight of her: flushed and glistening with sweat, neck arched in abandon.

"You feel so perfect," I groan against her ear, nipping at her lobe before trailing kisses down her neck, leaving a path of goosebumps in their wake. My hammering heartbeat echoes in my ears, synchronized with the wet, slick sounds of our bodies coming together. "So unbelievably perfect."

Anya's response is lost in a moan as she writhes beneath me, hips bucking against mine as she clings to the edge of the mattress. Her fingers tangle in the sheets, straining against the fabric as if it were my skin. She's close, I can tell by the desperate way her body quivers around me, and that knowledge only spurs me on more.

I growl against her swollen lips before suckling on her bottom lip gently. The combination of pleasure and pain tips her over the edge and she arches off the bed, nails leaving white-hot lines on my back as she cries out my name.

My voice comes out raw with desperation. "Anya, I *need* to claim you..." I rasp against her neck. "I want *all* of you... Oh, gods!" My body quakes with uncontrollable desire. I can't stop myself anymore. I must mark her as mine, to leave an indelible brand on her silken skin that will last an eternity.

"Yes...!" she responds with a sultry moan, giving herself over to me completely.

With one final, powerful thrust, I surge deep within her contracting depths and stiffen as my climax rocks through me, unyielding in its intensity. A primal roar escapes my lips as I release everything within her, claiming her as my mate, my blood bonded to hers for all eternity. The connection between us ignites like wildfire, searing and scorching as our orgasms crash together in a cacophony of passionate growls and whimpers.

My body trembles as the searing heat of my climax courses through my veins, a molten wave of pleasure, unlike anything I've ever experienced before. With a savage growl that is both animalistic and triumphant, I pull back just enough to angle myself more precisely, aligning my fangs with the throbbing vein at the slope of her shoulder. At once, the scent of her arousal and the heady scent of her blood fills my nostrils, clouding my already addled senses. My canines lengthen in anticipation, aching to taste that honey-sweet nectar that will seal our bond for eternity.

Anya whimpers under me, her breathing ragged and body trembling as she clings to me with all her might. "Take me... make me yours... I'm yours, Vlad..." she breathes out between pants, her words sending fire straight to my core. My self-control snaps like a taut bowstring in that moment, and with one last, powerful thrust, I plunge my fangs deep into her shoulder as I empty myself inside her.

Her blood coats my tongue like ambrosia, sweet and intoxicatingly rich. As our two hearts hammer against each other in a frantic rhythm, our blood mingles, intertwining our very souls as we collapse into each other's arms. We are no longer two separate beings but one. Bound together for eternity, entwined in a bond that transcends time.

Anya's whimpers of ecstasy mingle with mine as our orgasms subside, our bodies still joined as our pulses slow to a more manageable rhythm. She shivers beneath me, her nails still embedded in my back, and I can feel the searing heat of our bond solidifying between us like molten lava cooling into unbreakable obsidian.

Slowly, I pull my fangs from her shoulder, our gazes locking in the dim moonlight. Her eyes are now a swirling maelstrom of chestnut and amber, proof of the claiming that just took place. A smirk tugs at my lips as I brush a strand of hair from her face.

"Mine," I growl softly, my voice raw with emotion and possessiveness that I no longer have the will to hide. "You're mine, Anya."

Her eyes darken with desire and acceptance as she nods in agreement, her fingers tracing the wound that now bears the mark of my bite: a perfect pair of intertwined V and A symbols. "Through every lifetime... I belong to you...Vlad," she whispers hoarsely.

Gently, I lick the wound on her shoulder, speeding its healing before my eyes. And as we lay there, tangled in the sheets, our breathing gradually returning to normal, something inside me settles. A long-felt emptiness is finally filled, as if a missing piece of my very soul has been returned to me.

With a contented sigh, I roll onto my side, bringing her with me so she rests her head on my chest. Her heartbeat thuds against mine, a steady drumbeat that soothes the savage beast within me.

21
VLAD

The days pass in a blissful haze as Anya and I continue growing ever closer. Our new romance develops slowly but steadily, each shared moment forging fresh links in the profound bond between us.

My wounds have mended to faint scars thanks to Anya's mysterious healing powers. And she's finally finished the paintings commissioned by her patron Yulia before the roads become impassable.

We're preparing a simple dinner together in the kitchen when she mentions needing to deliver the artwork into town later today.

"I'd really like you to meet Yulia," she says. "She's quite a spectacular lady, truly one of a kind."

I pause in chopping vegetables to meet Anya's hopeful gaze. While social calls don't come naturally to me, I realize this trip is important to her. "I'm certain this Yulia must be quite special, to have earned such high praise from you," I reply.

Setting down the knife, I take Anya's delicate hand in my own and bring it to my lips in a tender kiss. Her blush as I do so never fails to make my inner wolf rumble with satisfaction. No matter how charming she finds this mentor, to me, Anya outshines all others.

"But you should know," I add throatily, "I've already had the privilege of meeting the most spectacular woman I'll ever know."

Anya melts beautifully at my sincerity, shyly meeting my eyes. In moments like this, her pure joy pierces through the darkness that once shrouded my battered soul. Each day with Anya is a gift, her light guiding me further out of lonely shadows into hope.

The urge to keep Anya confined safely in our territory gnaws at me as we prepare to venture out to her patron Yulia's estate. I know Anya values her independence, but ever since fate bound her to me as mate, my primal instincts bristle at letting her out of my sight. The wolf in me paces and snarls, fixated on shielding its vulnerable female. After my past failures, I cannot risk Anya coming to harm.

When she takes my hand reassuringly, sweetly trying to ease my restlessness, I feel a surge of gratitude and protectiveness. She does not fully grasp how utterly helpless I was when my old clan abandoned me, bleeding and broken in the snow. I will never allow Anya to know such devastation. She is *everything* to me—my hard-won second chance. I failed my kin, but I will tear apart anything that threatens my new mate.

The journey passes tensely as I scan our surroundings, senses primed for any potential threat. Anya stays close by my side, recognizing my need to keep her within reach. Her willingness to accommodate my instincts despite her independent spirit only deepens my longing to prove I can defend her against all perils.

As we approach the grand estate, a sense of foreboding settles in the pit of my stomach. The grounds are eerily silent, and my wolf senses pick up on a distinct absence of any other living beings nearby. Anya, unaware of my unease, rushes heedlessly forward.

"Stop!" I hiss, snatching her arm and pulling her to a halt.

She scowls at me, her expression darkening with confusion. "What's wrong?"

I scan our surroundings carefully before answering. "Something isn't right here," I say gravely.

Anya's eyes widen with worry as she looks around, finally noticing the strange stillness that hangs over the estate. She turns to me with determination in her eyes.

"I'm going to go check on Yulia," she declares, attempting to move past me.

I grab her arm again, firmly holding her back. "Wait here. I'll go first," I command, brooking no argument.

She frowns and opens her mouth to protest, but ultimately nods in agreement.

With a final warning look, I make my way towards the estate cautiously, scanning for any signs of danger or disturbance.

The minute I cross the threshold, it becomes clear to me that death and violence have tainted this place. Bloody claw marks score the walls, splintered furnishings discarded like broken toys. The metallic scent of fresh carnage hangs thick in the air. And at the end of the ruined hall lies the body.

Fury surges like lava in my veins. But my anger is swiftly replaced by increased wariness as I recognize the brutal attack comes not from man but beast. And the harrowing question pierces my blasted mind—is this Grisha's work? *It has to be.* And that can only mean one thing. He's been watching me all along, biding his time for his moment. This gruesome display is but a warning...

"No! Damn it!" I roar.

Anya's agonized scream slices through me. She shoves past me and runs to the savaged corpse. "Yulia! No, please gods, no!"

I grasp her shoulders firmly, trying to pull her back. "Look away, Anya," I urge through gritted teeth. But she won't be moved, weeping over her kind patron laid out in grisly desecration. Revulsion and rage churn sickly in my gut as I gaze down at the poor woman ripped so brutally from this world. And all because I was not strong enough to prevent it.

"We have to help her!" Anya sobs, lunging futilely towards the body. "We have to—"

Her knees buckle beneath her and I catch her in my arms, holding her steady with quiet authority. "She's gone, my heart. There's nothing we can do for her now. It's not safe here. We should leave."

When Anya continues resisting, I simply pick her up and stride for the exit. Getting distance between my mate and further danger is my sole imperative. Her safety eclipses my notions of dignity or honor.

As I spirit her away into the icy woods, a grim truth sinks into my bones. The malevolent threat we face is only growing stronger, and I do not yet have the strength or allies needed to conquer it. But for Anya, I will sacrifice anything, become anything necessary, to shield her from all harm. This much I know for certain.

I race onward until the grand manor disappears behind a veil of snow-laden pines, their denseness providing shelter. At last, I slow our headlong pace, setting Anya gently on her feet again though I keep one arm wrapped firmly around her. Her eyes are glazed, skin ice-pale with shock. Sheltering her shuddering frame in the cage of my arms, I stroke her hair, murmuring soft reassurances while scanning our surroundings for any sign of pursuit.

Abruptly, I go rigid, spine snapping straight. Foreign scents taint the crisp air, at least three unfamiliar wolves in our vicinity. I shift Anya protectively behind me, a vicious snarl rumbling in my chest loud as thunder.

"Show yourselves!" I bark, the command in my tone unmistakable. Any true wolf would recognize it instantly, an Alpha's decree that compels obedience.

There's a tense pause, then crackling footsteps crunch through the underbrush. Three male figures emerge warily into view between the barren trees. Their clothing is ragged and postures submissive, but it's the subtle elongated canines visible when they speak and the way their eyes reflect the light that reveals the truth—other wolf shifters like us.

My lips peel back instinctively, a vicious snarl rumbling in my chest. Every muscle coils, ready to strike down these trespassers in our territory. But I force patience. As an Alpha, I know the cost of attacking blindly before assessing whether they are potential allies or enemies.

The three keep their eyes lowered, baring their throats in submission. Lone wolves often prove more desperate and dangerous than those bonded to kin. I must discern their intentions with care before lowering my guard.

"Who are you?" I demand, infusing my tone with Alpha authority. "State your purpose."

The three exchange uneasy glances. The tallest, a muscular sandy-haired youth, finds his voice first. "We mean no threat. We came to help the old woman when we heard her screams, but arrived too late."

His comrades nod, shamefaced. "We could scent you and your mate had just come from there," the brawny one adds. "You *saw* what evil was done to her."

I study the ragged trio closely as they address me head-on. No guile or deceit lurks in their downturned eyes—only remorse. These are omega wolves, expendable runts of a pack who could not protect their own against a powerful enemy. Sympathy stirs grudgingly beneath my fury.

I close the distance, stare boring into them. "Tell me what you know of this attack. Now."

Behind me, Anya's grip on my hand tightens.

The shortest of the omegas glances anxiously at the others before speaking. "We were out hunting when the screams carried on the wind. We got there just as the pack was fleeing the manor, their leader dragging... dragging her body." He shudders.

"Who was he?" I snap, furious, as the harrowing scene flashes in my mind's eye.

The dark-eyed one's rough voice cuts through the tense silence, "Their Alpha bore a dagger and wolf emblem branded on his arm, and had hair pale as the snow. There were at least ten others as well."

I clench my fists tightly against the rage howling inside me. *Not Grisha*—this was an unknown Alpha's doing. But the brutality carries the same depraved message.

"Where is your pack? Your Alpha?" I question. "I would have words with them about strengthening our united numbers against this threat."

The three outcasts shift uneasily, refusing to meet my gaze. "We have no pack," the sandy-haired one admits. "We three are... lone wolves."

The admission makes my chest constrict painfully. I know too well the hardship of surviving solo without pack bonds.

A low growl rumbles in my throat. I exhale slowly, mind churning with this new information. If I am to combat this menacing evil, I will need allies. And these three lost souls may prove valuable indeed.

I turn to Anya and gently raise her chin until our eyes meet. Her gaze is clearing from its earlier shock, strength beginning to return. She searches my face trustingly.

"It seems fate has brought us and these young wolves together, just when we each need allies most," I say. Anya's eyes widen in understanding.

I turn back to the omegas, who fidget nervously. "My mate and I would welcome you three into our fold, if you would pledge yourselves to us and our purpose."

The trio stare in disbelief for a long stunned moment. Then as one, they drop to their knees before us in supplication. "We are forever in your debt," they murmur humbly.

A smile curves my lips as fierce satisfaction roars through me. The fight to come will be long and bloody. But perhaps with these new loyal warriors, our odds are finally improving.

22

ANYA

I stare sightlessly out the frosted kitchen window, hands wrapped around a cooling mug of untouched tea. Days have passed in a blur since the gruesome attack at Yulia's estate. My kind patron did not deserve such a brutal end, and the weight of survivor's guilt presses heavily on my heart.

If not for my presence in this town, she would likely still be alive, going about her vibrant life. Her death was no random tragedy as Vlad believes— indeed, it was a message. But not the one he initially suspected.

Ever since the attack, I've been lost in my thoughts, too frightened and shocked to speak. Vlad has noticed it too, but he's been mindful to grant me space as I sort out my emotions.

From the moment I heard the description of the enemy Alpha, and the dagger brand he carries, I knew this was no random tragedy. It was a living nightmare, come for me at last.

The Alpha behind poor Yulia's murder is none other than Roan Mikhailov, the depraved leader of my old clan, the Alpha Krov pack. The same monster who forced me to abandon everyone and everything I knew to escape his twisted desires.

Now it seems my bid for freedom has failed. Roan finally tracked me here, and his bloody message was clear—this new haven will offer me no safety. He will raze it and everyone I care for to the ground unless I return to him. I'm sure he's not forgiven me for escaping his fangs on the night of my branding. He left me little choice, since he wouldn't reject me as his mate.

I thought a quiet life in the country would keep me safe from Roan's reach... How wrong I was.

This bitter knowledge has paralyzed my tongue, but I cannot conceal the truth from Vlad forever. Roan will not stop until I'm back under his cruel thumb or all I love lies in ruins. Either I find the courage to fight at last, or surrender to the merciless fate from which I once fled.

Heavy footsteps sound outside the kitchen,

followed by low voices. In the parlor, Vlad is speaking with our new pack members, the omega wolves who have pledged their loyalty. Word of an emerging sanctuary here has spread quickly, and now more lost wolves come seeking the shelter of pack daily. Our numbers swell, though it does little to ease the hollow ache inside me.

I pause outside the closed kitchen door. Vlad's deep rumbling voice drifts through the aged wood, locked in serious discussion with someone—one of our new pack members, by the sounds of it.

I hesitate, not wanting to intrude. But the urgency in their hushed tones intrigues me. I know I shouldn't eavesdrop, yet my feet remain rooted by the door, curiosity winning out.

Pressing nearer, I catch the tail end of Vlad's sentence. "...best thing you could do under the circumstances, don't you agree?"

"You're absolutely right," comes the fervent reply, tone laden with both relief and respect. I can't place the voice—perhaps Thane, one of the omega wolves who recently joined our ranks.

I hear movement within, and risk cracking the door slightly to peek through. Thane rises from the sofa, clasping Vlad's hand with effusive gratitude. "I feel much better about my options now."

Their exchange confuses me. The solitary man who stumbled bleeding into my life seems to be commanding greater followers by the day, all drawn to him by an unexplainable pull. It's almost as if Vlad were...

"Thank you for the counsel, *Alpha*," Thane says as he opens the door.

Vlad meets him on the threshold, giving his shoulder a reassuring pat. "I'll see you tonight at the strategy meeting."

I reel back from the door, pulse racing. *Alpha?* Vlad never mentioned being an alpha wolf, let alone leading his own pack—his brother Gavriil *was* the Alpha, the leader of the bear shifters... The mug slips from my quivering hand and shatters on the floor.

Within seconds, the door swings open, and Vlad ducks into the kitchen, his intense stormy eyes immediately finding me. "Is everything alright?" he rumbles softly.

My gaze meets his in uneasy silence. I bend down and start gathering the broken porcelain pieces scattered at my feet. "Yeah..." I breathe weakly.

Suddenly, Vlad kneels before me. His large, gentle hand encircles my slim wrist, stilling my nervous motions. "Anya...?" he purrs, leaning in, his earthy, masculine scent enveloping me.

I exhale sharply as the truth crystallizes in my mind. Eyes locked with his, I blurt out, "An Alpha... You're an Alpha?"

"I am," Vlad states simply, his stare boring into me.

My breaths come faster as I process this revelation. "When you spoke of your pack in Rome, you really meant *your* pack, because you were—*are*—the Alpha." He never outright deceived me about his status. Everything in me goes taut, a storm of emotions clashing inside.

"Hey now, easy..." Vlad's voice turns soothing, his free hand coming up to glide along my tense jawline. "I bet the untamed wolf in you wants to bolt and start running away right now, doesn't she?" he asks knowingly.

I inhale deeply and manage to regain some control over my visceral panic. "Maybe?" I whisper shakily.

"Well... don't," Vlad says, firm but gently commanding. "There's nothing here to run from, my love. Listen, so much has happened so fast between us. I understand this might feel like too much to handle right now."

He's right. Grief, pain, joy, and sheer dread of

losing this bond tangle tightly in my core. I cannot find the words to open my guarded heart to Vlad, to articulate these overwhelming emotions. After so long holding my walls up in isolation, I scarcely recall how it feels to let someone in fully.

Vlad's fingers under my chin draw my eyes back to his patient grey ones. His gaze narrows, reading my poorly concealed distress easily. "Talk to me, Anya," he urges, voice dropping into a gentle croon. "You've been so distant since the attack. I know you're grieving the loss of Yulia. But this unease in you runs deeper... I *feel* it." He inches closer, his breath laced with the scent of mint as it caresses my cheek. "You don't have to be alone in this anymore, my lovely wolf. Whatever haunts you, let me help carry the burden."

My throat tightens with emotion. Vlad means so well, but he does not fully comprehend the true scope of the bloody shadow now looming over us. I should confess everything, but panic has my tongue frozen.

Vlad's steady hands come up to cup my face, forcing me to meet his stare. "We are mates now, you and I," he says firmly. "Your trials are mine to share. Please, trust me as I trust you."

His earnest plea breaks my paralysis at last. I

cannot keep avoiding this forever, though the truth may destroy the haven I've found with Vlad. But the time has come to stop hiding from my past demons.

Eyes burning, I swallow hard and prepare myself to speak my truth. His fingers lace through mine, grounding me as I gather frayed composure. Ready or not, I have to come clean—at this point, it would be reckless not to.

Finally, in halting words, I paint the whole wretched picture—my history with the Alpha Krov pack, their brutal leader's interest, and the only means left to me to escape his sadistic desires.

"Yulia's death was a warning, Vlad," I explain. "From *him*. He finally tracked me here." Unshed tears clog my throat.

Vlad's expression blackens with fury and pain on my behalf as understanding dawns. "Who is it?" he grates out. "Give me this beast's name."

I close my eyes, seeing again the handsome youth who morphed into a monster right in front of me. "Roan Mikhailov. Leader of the Alpha Krov pack."

A litany of curses in Russian erupts from Vlad as he surges to his feet. For a moment I brace myself, expecting his blinding rage and fury to overwhelm him. But when his blazing eyes find mine again, they hold steely purpose instead of madness.

"That monster will never lay a finger on you again. I swear it on my life," Vlad vows, his words razor-edged. "He and every last one of his depraved pack will suffer and pay for aiding his twisted desires."

Despite the icy fear still choking me, Vlad's fervent promise kindles a fragile ember of hope beneath my breastbone. I rise on trembling legs to join him, brushing tentative fingers over his clenched, white-knuckled fist.

"We will face him together," I manage to whisper. Lifting my chin, I meet Vlad's stare unflinchingly. "I won't run or hide any longer."

A fierce light enters Vlad's eyes at my quiet bravery. Vlad crushes me against the solid bulk of his chest in answer. I cling to him, letting our shared strength leach away some of my paranoia. Whatever comes, I will not stand alone against the demon from my past again. With my brave mate and our growing numbers at my side, hope flickers weakly.

A sharp rap at the front door startles us apart. Wiping my eyes hastily, I follow Vlad to the foyer where one of our omega wolves lingers on the threshold speaking with a stranger. Their voices carry to us in snatches through the cracked door.

"...never met, but I heard you might help..."

"The Alpha will decide."

"Please, I have nowhere else..."

Vlad strides forward out into the falling snow, assessing the ragged newcomer with a piercing stare. I hang back in the doorway, pulse kicking. More refugees come daily, but something about this one makes my skin prickle ominously. His scent... so familiar. Dread rises like bile in my throat.

As if sensing my presence, the stranger turns. His cruel eyes meet mine over Vlad's shoulder, and my vision narrows to his leering visage. Even with brutal scars marring one side of his face, I recognize him instantly. *Boris, one of Roan's enforcers.*

Vlad must feel me sway on my feet. He whirls, questions in his eyes, but Boris is faster. With viper speed, he slashes a silver dagger from his belt and plunges it into Vlad's broad chest.

"NOOO!" My agonized scream shreds the air. Vlad's face contorts in shock and pain before he drops heavily to his knees.

Boris wrenches back his bloodied blade, sneering at my horror. "You shouldn't have run, little wolf," he growls. "But now, you're coming home."

He lunges for me, fetid exhale hot on my skin. Then Koen, our omega guard is there, form rippling as snapping jaws close on Boris' arm in a spray of crimson. His shriek mingles with my own as I fall to Vlad's side, pressing my hands desperately against the blood-red stain spreading on his shirt.

"Vlad, look at me!" I plead over the sounds of the scuffle behind us. Hazy grey eyes meet mine, face deathly pale beneath the blood.

"Run..." he rasps, "...safe..."

Then his eyes roll back and his body convulses. My wrenching sobs fill the entryway now painted with gore. I scarcely register the ominous silence until a heavy hand clamps down on my shoulder.

"Time to go home now, bitch," Boris' mocking voice croons in my ear.

I don't fight as he hauls me upright, Vlad's blood slick on my palms. All will burn to ash in the face of my failure. I couldn't protect Yulia from my past, and now Vlad lies dying because of my silence. Perhaps this is simply the fate I deserve.

Numbness engulfs me, Boris' taunting voice fading to meaningless noise as he drags me forcibly into the silver forest and whatever fresh horrors await. I left a trail of pain in my futile bid for freedom. Now there will be a reckoning at Roan's hands. And I no longer have any will left to resist or flee the vengeance coming for me.

Heartbroken and shocked, I go limply without protest, leaving behind my slain love and the ruins of all we worked to build together. The cold bitterness of the coming night feels fitting. I'm ready to surrender to the darkness once more...

23
ANYA

Consciousness returns reluctantly through the pounding ache in my skull. I peel open my gritty eyes to total darkness. The hard-packed earth under my cheek reeks of dampness and mold, fetid water trickling somewhere nearby. I seem to be lying on the floor of some lightless cellar or cave. Clammy air clings to my skin, chilled and stale from lack of circulation.

Shifting my protesting limbs, I feel jarring metal bite into my wrists—shackles chained to the unforgiving wall behind me. Another clamping vise of iron encircles my throat, chained to the floor to restrain the rabid she-wolf within. Panic grips my chest, breaths sawing harshly in the oppressive blackness.

Where am I? What fresh hell have my demons dragged me into now?

Memory comes creeping back as my vision adjusts by agonizing degrees to the lightless space. The attack at our haven, Vlad's body stabbed by Boris' cruel blade before they ripped me from his side… A broken cry of grief escapes my raw throat as the scene replays in gruesome detail.

Oh, Moon Goddess. My beloved Vlad. Please let his end have come swiftly, without needless suffering. The likelihood he survived such viciousness is vanishingly small. My soul ruptures anew imagining his final moments believing I fled willingly, leaving him to die alone.

The force of inconsolable heartache over losing my mate, my entire world, nearly doubles me over. I grit my teeth against the building scream, choking it back through sheer stubbornness. I must believe that wherever Vlad is, he knows I would have given my last breath to save him. That wild hope is all that keeps my shattered heart beating now.

A sudden flare of harsh light makes me flinch as the small cellar is illuminated. Boris leans casually against the far earthen wall, puffing languidly on a cigarette. His mangled face splits in a revolting grin when he notices I'm conscious.

"There she is. The traitorous little whore," he rasps, pushing off the wall to approach my crumpled form. I shrink back instinctively from his menacing bulk. Boris' grin widens at my fear.

"Finally decided to join us… eh, princess?" He takes a long, exaggerated drag on the cigarette, then blows the acrid smoke directly into my face. I recoil, coughing as the noxious cloud envelops me.

Boris crouches down, forcing me to meet his malignant stare. "Was starting to think I hit you too hard during our little trip. Would be a shame if you never got to enjoy your long overdue homecoming."

It all comes crashing back at his mocking words —we must be somewhere on the expansive territory still claimed by the Alpha Krov pack, my prison long ago. A different cell, but the same sadistic warden.

I force my features to stillness, refusing to gratify this beast by showing any reaction. But maintaining a disaffected facade takes every ounce of my will when Vlad's beloved, rugged face fills my mind once more. The very air feels lodged solidly in my lungs, refusing to move.

"What's this now? No tears or pleas for your lost sweetheart?" Boris scoffs. "Don't you care at all that he died bloody and alone?"

His cruel goading hits its mark. The thought of

Vlad drawing his last agonized breaths believing I abandoned him is unendurable. He was everything to me—my heart, my redemption. And he perished thinking I had callously forsaken him when he needed me most.

Something in me snaps at last. "Vlad was worth a hundred of a vile coward like you," I spit venomously. "He was loyal, brave and true. And you cut him down like a rabid dog!"

Chest heaving, I bare my teeth at Boris in lupine fury, uncaring of the consequences. "So, kill me too if you want. Because I will never stop trying to avenge him, you foul beast. Not if I have to chase you straight to the depths of hell!"

My venomous words seem to rock Boris back a step. But quickly, the cruel smirk returns to his ruined face. "Still plenty of fire left in you after all," he chuckles darkly. "Good. Our Alpha will *so* enjoy beating it out..."

I can't help but wince, feeling hot tears forming in my eyes. I must cling to the frail hope that perhaps Vlad's grievous wound was not fatal. With his advanced shifter healing, maybe his new followers found and aided Vlad before his spirit fled this world. Surely he realized in those final moments that I would never willingly leave his side, no matter the consequences.

This thin thread of faith in the power of our bond is the only thing keeping my shattered psyche from giving way completely. So long as it remains, I can endure whatever else is coming. I must if I ever hope to get back to Vlad.

The rough dirt floor trembles under approaching footfalls, heralding another's arrival. My empty stomach roils with dread as the hulking silhouette of a broad-shouldered man fills the crude doorway. Even awash in shadows, I recognize that confident posture, the entitled tilt of his head. Revulsion instantly scorches away my grief and despair, replaced by bone-deep rage.

"There she is, my sweet little Stasia." Roan's mocking endearment heralds his entrance into my squalid prison. My former pack name on his lips shoots a shiver down my spine. "It seems you and I still have some unfinished business between us, darling."

He dismisses the smirking Boris with a derisive flick of his wrist. My pulse hammers as Roan begins to circle my huddled form with languid purpose. I brace myself for explosive violence, but he merely watches me with predatory amusement. The way his gaze roams my body, however, makes my skin crawl as if coated in filth.

When Roan inhales deeply, eyelids briefly sinking closed, I taste bile at the back of my throat. "Just as delicious as I recall," he purrs. "Absconding from your Alpha could not change that."

The possessive words ignite my temper. I waited years for any chance to escape this beast's clutches, nearly losing myself entirely in the process. Yet he still believes I am nothing more than a plaything to be bent to his twisted desires.

"I stopped belonging to you the day I ran away from this prison," I spit venomously.

Roan's eyes flare crimson at my defiance, but his retaliation is controlled, almost languid. He casually backhands me across the face, splitting my lip and filling my mouth with the coppery tang of blood.

"We'll soon cure you of that insolent tongue once more." Roan grasps my jaw, nails digging into my skin. "This time, you will not escape your branding. Then, you'll serve your true purpose here as brood-mare for my heirs—once I've disciplined that fiery will again."

His vile threat makes my stomach roil. I barely restrain the urge to vomit on his expensive Italian loafers. But I refuse to show any reaction that might satisfy his sadism, staring stonily ahead.

Seeming to sense my silent rebellion regardless, Roan crouches until we are eye to eye. He trails one clawed fingertip down the slender column of my throat in a perverse caress.

"This is for your own good, little one. Obedience will earn you rewards again." His touches turn rougher, proprietary, when I try jerking away. "The comforts you grew accustomed to before you betrayed me so cruelly."

Memories of those "comforts"—privileges dangled before me like bones before a dog, keeping me tethered by fear and dependency—make me tremble with loathing.

Sneering at my disgust, Roan twists my hair brutally in his fist until pained tears spring forth despite my resolve. He forces my gaze back to him, eyes ablaze with sadistic promise.

"You will learn to appreciate my generous affections once more. I'll make sure of it." He kisses me with bruising force, reopening the split in my swollen lower lip. I endure his assault, motionless, until he relents at last.

Roan strokes my battered face almost tenderly

before releasing me. "We have difficult but rewarding work ahead, you and I. Very soon, all will be mended." He smiles, cold and nauseatingly certain. "I promise."

With those chilling parting words, Roan turns his back on me and strides from the dismal chamber. In the doorway, his silhouette pauses to rake one final possessive, devouring look over my huddled form. Then the heavy door slams shut, sealing me in pitch blackness once more.

Alone on the freezing dirt, still dazed from pain and fear, I can do nothing but weep bitterly. The full horror of my situation crashes down, forcing out harsh, broken sounds from my ravaged soul. However narrowly I managed to escape Roan's sadistic obsession before, this time there may be no way out of the lavish prison forged by his "love."

Eventually, no more tears come, my body and spirit drained. Curled against the cold wall, I desperately try conjuring every fading image of happiness and light found in Vlad's arms. But they bring only fresh waves of anguish now. That sweet dream of freedom and love has died along with the girl who dared hope for a future.

Whatever I face next in this unending nightmare, it will be with the hollowed-out shell that remains. The defiant flame within me has been extinguished, leaving behind only ashen remnants and darkness. Perhaps that is precisely what my jailer desires most, in the end—not just my body enslaved, but my soul shattered completely. And this time, he may finally achieve that sinister goal.

24

VLAD

I'm adrift in a sea of darkness, no light or sound to orient myself. But strangely, no pain either. Just... nothingness. Is this what it means to slip free of mortal bonds and into the eternal unknown?

A familiar distant melody seems to ripple through the void around me. A lilting folk song our old nursemaid sang while I played in the sun-warmed gardens of father's grand estate. The nostalgia kindles a spark deep within my benumbed spirit.

Gradually, the oppressive darkness recedes. In fleeting moments, sensation returns. The smoothness of a plush mattress beneath me. The ache of a ravaged body pushed beyond endurance. I cling to each discomfort, using them to pull my way up from the brink of oblivion.

With great effort, I force my leaden eyelids open. Blurred shapes hover over me, backlit by soft amber light. I make out dark hair and wide, concerned eyes the color of rich dark chocolate. Recognition stirs in me sluggishly.

"...Samara?" I rasp through cracked lips. My sister's heart-shaped face crumples in relief at the hoarse whisper. No illusion or cruel trick—somehow, impossibly, my little sister sits at my side. But how, and why here, in this secluded place?

"Shh... Try to rest, Volodya." Samara presses a cup to my mouth, coaxing me to drink the cool herbal draught. "You've been gravely hurt, but the worst has passed. I'll have you mended soon enough."

Her assurances wash over me, meaningless noise. My mind reels, trying to make sense of it all. The attack, Anya's pale and anguished face ripped away into darkness, my life bleeding out crimson onto the snow. By all rights, I should have perished. So, how is it that I'm still drawing breath?

With tremendous effort, I force the question past my dry throat. "What... what happened? What are you doing here?"

Samara's fine brows knit together. "*Healing you*, of

course," she snaps wryly. "I arrived just in time, it seems. That dagger missed your heart by a hair." Her voice catches slightly. "Good gods, Volodya… we thought we'd lost you in those woods, and now this."

Shame wells up, bitter as bile. Of course, they would assume me dead. I abandoned my clan to vengeful enemies, wounded beyond any hope. I do not deserve my sister's gentle attention or the relief in her eyes.

She purses her lips, a glimpse of gloom surfacing in her sweet semblance. "Everyone back home assumed you were dead. But I knew better—it would take *more* than a mere scratch to end an Alexeev."

"Volkov…" I rasp weakly in correction. "I left that name behind when I abandoned my mantle."

Samara makes a derisive noise. "You're *still* my brother. Enough with the proud lone wolf act, okay?" Her tone gentles as she grips my hand. "Right now, you just need to focus on healing."

She's right. Anya remains in enemy hands while I lay here mending. The thought spurs me upright despite the vicious agony the motion causes. I hiss air through my teeth, hand going instinctively to the fresh bandages swathing my chest.

"Easy, Vlad!" Samara presses me back firmly. Her palm glows rose-gold with healing magic and blessed numbness spreads through my wound. But it cannot touch the deeper pain gnawing at me.

"I have to find Anya," I grit out. "Before they hurt her..."

Understanding fills Samara's eyes. "The girl who saved you?"

"My... mate," I clarify, my voice laced with possessiveness.

Sam readjusts my bandage. The pressure against the tender injury beneath steals a growl from me.

"Hey, now. No biting," she chides with a playful smirk, then runs her fingers through my hair. "You *will* find her, once your strength returns. And thanks to my skills, that won't take long." A smug wink seals the deal.

Sam's customary confidence bolsters my flagging spirit. She was always the most gifted among our clan's witch kin, wielding power beyond her years. With her aid, perhaps I can still wrest Anya from our foes' clutches and protect what we've built together.

Samara helps prop me upright against the bed's headboard, fussing over my many scars until I wave off her concerns. There is too much still unexplained between us. I must understand how she came to be here when by all accounts I should have faced death alone.

"How the hell did you get here without anyone in the clan knowing?" I blurt out.

My sister's gaze drops to the ground. She nibbles on her lower lip, clearly stalling for an answer.

"Sam?" I press, my impatience boiling over.

She lets out a heavy sigh. "Oh… alright," she says. "Officially, I'm supposed to be at my friend Mila's dacha, taking some time away to clear my head."

"You shouldn't have risked yourself finding me, Samara. It was foolishly dangerous for you to leave the clan's territory." Even as I scold her recklessness, gratitude swells within me. However she managed it, my sister saved my life with her selfless bravery.

Sam flashes a wry smile. "Finding people is what I do best, if you'll recall. And you should know better than to think I'd leave my own kin for dead." Sobriety replaces her playful expression. "We mourn you back home, Vlad. Losing both you and Luciana has devastated us all—*especially* Gavriil."

My breath catches painfully. "Gavriil… he still lives?" Cautious hope stirs from the ashes. Perhaps not all is lost, if my wild young brother yet walks this earth.

"I wouldn't call it living," Samara says with a sigh, her eyes turning melancholy. "It's more like *surviving*. He has changed so much since the loss of his mate…

He roams more beast than man now beyond our borders. And when he's home, I struggle to control his fury."

I stare at nothing, guilt and remorse churning. My disappearance has clearly inflicted deep wounds upon what remains of my family. But before I can dwell further, Samara grips my arm demandingly.

"Brother, look at me." When I meet her fierce gaze, she continues. "There is still time to set right what has gone awry. But first, we must save your mate and have you restored as Alpha." Her gaze drifts towards the hallway, where my newfound pack warily lingers, waiting for news. "This pack needs your steady hand."

I start to protest that I failed my pack utterly, how can I hope to lead a new one? But Samara talks over me. "Enough! The gods spared you for a reason. There is still work ahead." She holds my stare challengingly until I concede with a jerky nod.

"Good. It's settled." Brisk once more, Samara hands me a small crimson vial. "Drink this. It will help rebuild your strength." She pauses, her eyes flashing with determination. "We've preparations to make before we rescue your love from those good-for-nothing wolves."

I accept the potion, but hesitation roots me in

place. Doubt coils insidiously despite her assurances. The path ahead is treacherous, demanding much blood. And Anya's life hangs precariously in the balance. What if I falter again when she needs me most?

Sensing my inner turmoil, Sam sighs. She lifts my hand, pressing a kiss to the black bear insignia tattooed on my inner wrist—an oath of allegiance to my Ursa family. "One step at a time, Volodya. Have courage, brother."

The gentle command bolsters me enough to tip the potion down my raw throat. Fiery energy immediately spreads through my battered body, the first healing tingles of magic. I will need every drop of strength for what is to come. But with my witch-sister's aid, perhaps we can still win this war.

I keep hold of Samara's slender hand, meeting her stalwart gaze. To speak my swelling emotions seems inadequate. But she understands the depths of my gratitude, regardless. Of all the unlikely blessings fate could have granted me in this bleak hour, having my wise sister here feels like deliverance.

Together, with Samara's unshakable faith and my pack's unwavering support, we will accomplish what I could not alone. And soon, I will rescue Anya from the dark beast that took her. Of that, I silently vow, there is no question. No power, earthly or damned, could keep me from reclaiming my beloved and making our enemies pay in blood.

"Help me up, Sam…" I groan.

My sister's shoulder braces me as I struggle to unbend my battered body and stand. The simple action drains what little reserves I've regained, but I stubbornly stay upright.

Samara's smile holds pride and promise. "There's the brother I know. Come on—we've much to do and very little time."

Side by side, we leave the room that sheltered me from death's edge. The cozy walls fall away, revealing a bustle of activity in our lair beyond. My pulse quickens, battle singing in my veins once more. With my sister's magic and my lethal fury, our foes will soon learn to rue the day they crossed us.

The real fight begins now.

The rusted iron bolt screeches in protest as the heavy wooden door separating me from the manor above swings outward. I recoil instinctively from the slash of sunlight cutting through the darkness, raising a trembling hand to shield my sensitive eyes.

How long have I been condemned to this windowless cellar? Days and nights blur together in an endless torment of hunger, cold, and isolation. My world has contracted to the few cramped feet of moldy straw and crumbling stone surrounding me. The only interruptions are when Boris descends the steps to toss moldy bread scraps at my feet, more to torment than nourish.

"Get up, now." Boris' gruff voice echoes off the

slick stone walls beaded with moisture. "The Alpha has summoned you."

Primal fear slithers down my spine at those words, turning my empty stomach. Roan only ever calls me forth from my underground prison for one purpose —to humiliate and degrade me, attempting to crush the last embers of defiance that still smolder deep within.

So far, I have managed to cling to these tattered shreds of pride, refusing to completely submit to his will. But each hateful encounter leaves me more hollowed out and despairing inside. How much longer until he succeeds in breaking me fully?

The shackles enclosing my raw wrists clank as Boris hauls me to my feet. I stand unsteadily, legs cramped and weak from lack of use. With a firm shove between my shoulder blades, he forces me up the uneven stone steps into the manor, blinding light assaulting my dilated pupils.

As my vision adjusts, I take in the opulent surroundings that are so foreign after my confinement —intricate silk damask wallpaper, massive gilded mirrors in elaborate frames reflecting the crystal chandeliers glittering above. This manor embodies the immense wealth and influence the Alpha Krov pack has accumulated through generations of cruelty and bloodshed.

"Get her cleaned up before presenting her to the Alpha." Boris pushes me towards a pretty beta girl standing demurely with an armful of luxurious fabrics and soaps. "And make it quick, girl."

I stand numbly, swaying with exhaustion as the beta hurries to strip the filthy rags from my body. She clucks under her tongue at my pitiful state. Had it not been for her kind eyes, I would have recoiled from her touch. But her movements are efficient yet gentle as she scrubs the layers of grime from my gaunt frame, the linen clothes rough against my hypersensitive skin.

The girl pours fragrant oils into the tangled mass of hair hanging limply past my bony shoulders, working through the knots with an ivory-handled brush until it shines like spun copper. My scalp tingles painfully under her ministrations after going so long without proper care.

At last, she holds up an oval looking glass, silently inviting me to inspect her handiwork. I blink slowly, struggling to reconcile the haunted waif staring back at me with my self-image. Sunken cheeks streaked with dirt, limp hair hanging in lank strands, the sharp press of ribs beneath parchment-like skin...

only the eyes are the same, completely devoid of hope.

I stand submissively as the beta drapes the luxurious red silk dress over my frame, the neckline cut revealingly low. Bile burns in the back of my throat as her clever fingers do up the line of tiny buttons down the back. I am a plaything, stripped of my free will and dolled up for my captor's twisted enjoyment.

Too soon, Boris returns, his meaty paw closing around my slender upper arm as he propels me down the carpeted hallway towards an elaborate set of gilded double doors. My pulse thrums rapidly beneath my skin, breaths coming quicker in anticipation of the torment ahead.

At my throat, the hateful collar chafes, the metal engraved with runes to prevent any attempt to shift forms. Roan will take no chances—I might try to tap into my wolf's strength and speed to attempt escape.

The doors swing open soundlessly at our approach. Boris' grip acts like a vise, half dragging me into the lavishly appointed study. Behind an imposing mahogany desk, Roan reclines lazily in a leather chair, though his hooded gaze is alert and predatory.

"Ah… my lovely Stasia." His smile is a cruel twist of thin lips as Boris forces me before the desk. "You look absolutely ravishing."

His piercing eyes trail over me slowly while I stare straight ahead, jaw clenched with the effort not to tremble. I do not react. I will not give him the sick satisfaction of seeing my fear.

With an idle snap of his elegant fingers, Roan gestures for Boris to bring forth a silver platter from the sideboard, laden with a decadent spread—juicy roasted pheasant, creamy potatoes swimming in butter, crackers piled high with glistening black caviar.

The rich aromas hit my empty stomach like a physical blow. When have I last eaten anything beyond moldy crusts of bread and brackish water? I can feel my traitorous mouth flooding with saliva, my body instinctively craving nourishment after prolonged deprivation.

"You must be positively famished after your... accommodations," Roan purrs, his smile growing as he watches me struggle not to betray my desperation. "I can't have my pet wasting away to nothing now, can I?"

He plucks a plump green grape between two fingers and holds it up to my cracked lips in mocking offering. Revulsion churns within at being hand-fed like an animal, but the ravenous creature inside me cannot resist after so long without real food.

I bite down hesitantly, the tart sweetness of the fruit flooding my mouth and bringing involuntary tears to my eyes. I chew slowly, loathing myself and Roan with equal fierceness for this humiliation.

"There, now. That wasn't so difficult." Roan's smug pleasure is all but tangible. He continues placing morsels of the feast into my mouth—succulent pheasant flesh, slivers of creamy cheese, goose liver melted on the tongue. Like a master rewarding a dog for performing a trick well.

My stomach roils and heaves, but I force myself to continue swallowing everything he gives me. I will need whatever strength the meal provides for the true battle of wills ahead. Let Roan believe this small submission means I am broken.

When the last crumb has disappeared, Roan dismisses Boris with a flick of his fingers. My heart stutters as he rises and moves languidly around the desk. I stare straight ahead at the paneled wall, screams echoing silently in my mind as he comes to stand just behind me.

His hands trail lightly over my bare shoulders, eliciting an involuntary shudder as my skin crawls. Slowly, those hands move down my arms and come to rest possessively on my waist, gripping tightly. I can feel his hot breath stirring the hair by my neck as he leans in, inhaling my scent like an animal.

Suddenly, his fingers dig painfully into my side. "What's this?" he hisses. I shudder as his fingertips trace the magical brand on my shoulder blade—the intricate letter V intertwined with an A, marking me as Vlad's true mate, though invisible to human eyes.

Roan's voice drips fury. "You dared be claimed by another?"

He spins me around roughly to face him, eyes burning with rage. "That pathetic excuse for an Alpha could not protect what was his. You belong to *me* now."

His grip turns bruising once more. "You see, Anastasia? With proper discipline, even a wild creature can learn obedience." His fingers dig into my neck cruelly. "I've given you food and finery. Your only purpose now is to serve my desires without question. Refuse again, and you'll yearn for the comforts of your cellar."

Something at my core ignites, momentarily overriding the fog of fear and desperation that has numbed me. With a feral snarl, I whirl in his grasp, raking my nails violently across his smug face and grasping for his cold eyes.

We grapple fiercely, upending the desk as he

swears and tries to restrain my explosion of malice. I bite and claw like a cornered wildcat, beyond reason now. In my madness, I know only the desire to maim and disfigure.

The struggle is short-lived. Roan quickly overpowers me, using his superior size and weight to force me down against the lush carpet. I pant harshly, vision tinged with red as he rises above me, dabbing gingerly at the deep scratches marring his sharp cheekbones.

"Worthless bitch." His voice is deadly soft. He draws back a heavy fist adorned with rings and strikes me with brutal force. My head jerks sharply to the side, coppery blood filling my mouth. Sickening lights dance behind my eyelids.

Roan stands smoothly, tugging his expensive suit back into place. Only the enraged gleam in his pale eyes betrays his controlled exterior.

In one quick move, he throws open the doors. "Take her back to the cellar," he says. "No food or water for three days." His lip curls in unveiled disgust. "Put the animal back in her proper cage."

Rough hands drag me back through those imposing doors, the fight utterly drained from my limbs. Once sealed below ground again, I collapse limply into the foul straw, trembling uncontrollably as reaction sets in.

Blood still drips from my swollen lip as I lay there. Tears carve hot trails through the grime on my cheeks. But even when brutally beaten and starved, that stubborn flame deep inside my soul still flickers, refusing to be extinguished fully.

In the lonely darkness, I mentally prepare for the next inevitable summons above ground. When Boris comes for me again, I will be docile and compliant, luring Roan into believing I am well and truly tamed.

Let the arrogant fool think he has succeeded in crushing my spirit where all others failed. Like any predator, he can never anticipate his prey might turn and bite the hand that fed. I will play the role of a captive pet, awaiting my opportunity.

My thoughts turn to fantasies of slipping a hidden dagger between his ribs, stealing the very breath from his lungs as crimson blossoms across his crisp white shirt. Or letting a slow-acting poison seep into his evening wine until he chokes on his own blackened tongue...

I harbor no delusions about the probable outcomes. These vengeance-filled daydreams will likely only end in my own tortured death should I act them out. But at this point, without my beloved mate by my side, I hold my life as worthless.

Perhaps it is madness brought on by isolation and despair, but that stubborn flame of defiance fixates on imagining every possible way I might still end Roan's despicable life, even at the cost of my own. If only I could know Vlad has found some measure of justice...

So, I retreat deep within the recesses of my mind, building up my hatred into a roaring bonfire. Roan's arrogance will inevitably become his downfall. And on that day, be it near or far, I will be ready and waiting to strike the fatal blow.

For now, I can be patient. My time will come.

26

VLAD

bitter wind howls through the snow-flecked forest, whipping my fur and clawing icy fingers through my thick coat. I pay it no mind, focused solely on the looming fortress visible through the barren trees ahead. Roan's stronghold. My pulse thunders in anticipation of the coming battle. Tonight, my enemy will pay for everything he has done.

I raise a closed fist, halting my pack behind me. Pricked ears and bristling hackles reflect the disturbance I sense ahead—we are not alone out here. Dropping into a crouch, I scan the shadowed woods, every sense straining. We have crossed deep into Roan's territory, where discovery means swift death.

With quick hand signals, I motion for my pack to

214

fan out, encircling whatever lies ahead. Silent as smoke, they melt into the darkness. I creep forward alone, paws soundless in the fresh powder. The noises grow louder—crunching snow, snapping branches. The rhythm tugs at my memory. Strange, yet also familiar...

I sink into a hunting stance, ready to strike. My powerful muscles coil, then release, as I sail through the concealing underbrush. I land in a crouch behind the hulking figure, my knife instantly at its throat.

"It's me, brother," comes a rough whisper.

Shock roots me in place. The knife clatters forgotten to the snowy ground. As I straighten, the figure turns—*Enrico*, my most trusted enforcer. Joy and disbelief war within me.

"Enrico? What are you doing here?" I demand in a harsh whisper.

His eyes gleam with emotion in the moonlight. "Searching for you, Alpha. Since you disappeared, we've been half-mad with worry, scouring the land for some sign of your whereabouts."

Around us, my Roman pack emerges from hiding, yipping and gasping at this reunion. I clasp arms with Enrico, overwhelmed. Loyal to the last, they never stopped looking for me.

"How did you find me?" I have to ask.

"Your sister Samara sent us your location," Enrico explains with a shrug.

I can't help but smile. My witchy sister knows more than one way to work her magic.

As we embrace, the rest of my Roman pack also steps out from the shadows, until we are surrounded by our combined forces. For the first time since this nightmare started, hope surges within me. With our two packs united as one, we will be unstoppable. Enrico meets my gaze and nods firmly, a silent promise that we will fight to the death to defeat our common enemy tonight.

"Brothers, listen!" Enrico addresses the crowd. "We know the Alpha Krov pack holds our Luna captive." His face hardens with resolve. "The time has come to unite and take back what is ours."

Murmurs of assent ripple through the group. Enrico meets my gaze unwaveringly. "Command us, Alpha. We stand ready to fight and die at your side tonight."

Emotion constricts my throat. But with my pack beside me again, strength and purpose flow back into my veins. Together, we will be unstoppable.

I lift my head and let loose a bone-chilling howl that echoes through the silent woods. One by one, my wolves join in until our combined voices shake the very stars above. The final battle is at hand.

Under cover of darkness, we approach the towering manor house looming ahead. My hackles bristle with hatred for the beasts inside, and what depraved acts Anya may have suffered at their hands. Rage simmers in my blood, hungry for violence. I yearn to tear them all apart.

Crouching low, I swiftly outline the plan. At my signal, Enrico's unit will storm the front entrance as a distraction, while Thane's team scales the crumbling west wall. My warriors will infiltrate through the forested east wing. Surprise is our greatest weapon. We must be swift and merciless.

Enrico grips my shoulder, eyes blazing gold. "This night heralds the downfall of our enemies. Anya will be safe again before dawn."

I meet his feral gaze and nod. Then, with lightning speed, I bound forward and launch myself up and over the high stone wall in a single graceful leap. I land in a silent crouch amidst the deserted gardens. Soft footfalls behind me signal my team has cleared the wall after me. The stillness of the night settles heavily around us.

It's time.

I make my way swiftly across the grounds and slip

inside through an unguarded terrace door. As I creep down the darkened hallway, I spot a katana displayed prominently on the wall. I take the blade down, the well-oiled metal hissing free of its ebony sheath—Roan's own weapon, now turned against him.

At my signal, Thane's fighters scale the walls and tear into the flanked guards with savage fury. Gripping the katana, I lead the charge through the east wing, the singing blade spraying hot blood in a ruthless arc.

We are an unstoppable tidal wave, dealing swift death under the moon's cold light. No mercy for these monsters, no quarter given, only pure and savage vengeance. They have lived far too long already.

With each life I take, each cry silenced, my only thought is of reaching Anya. Is she here, somewhere in this labyrinth? Is she hurt, or worse? The possibilities fuel the berserker rage rising within me.

I reach out with my mind, trying to sense Anya through our mate bond. But I'm met only with deafening silence. Our connection is being blocked somehow. Dark magic must be at work here.

Still, I push the message into the void with all my might: *"I'm alive, Anya. I'm coming for you. Wait for me, my love."*

The silence persists, but I cannot give up hope.

Sword blade singing, I cut a ruthless path through Roan's minions, drawing ever nearer to where I now feel Anya's spirit resides. She cannot sense me, but I know exactly where to find her.

A guttural roar of fury echoes above the chaos. At the top of the grand staircase stands the hulking form of Roan, pale eyes burning with psychotic rage.

"You vermin dare invade my home?" he thunders. "I will bathe in your blood!"

He shifts into a massive grey wolf and charges down the steps, swatting aside my wolves like rag dolls. But I stand firm, blade leveled unwaveringly at my foe.

"This ends tonight, Roan."

With a bellow, he lunges. I spin nimbly aside, my sword carving a slash along his shoulder. He roars, lumbering around, but I am smoke on the wind. My katana flashes, a lethal streak of silver, biting into fur and flesh.

Blood sheets down Roan's heaving flanks. Yet still he comes on. A massive paw catches me across the ribs, launching me into a stone column. The air explodes from my lungs. I roll aside just as sledge-hammer blows shatter the marble where I lay seconds before.

On hands and knees, I suck desperate breaths,

ribs screaming in protest. Roan looms above, jaws gaping wide. *This is it.* With my last ounce of strength, I drive my blade upward, angling for his heart.

Suddenly, shouts and snarls erupt behind us. A dozen fighters from my pack converge on Roan, dragging the snarling wolf down under their combined weight.

I glance back to see Roan's massive wolf form disappear beneath a writhing pile of enemies. My warriors have him contained for now, but I must move quickly. Anya needs me.

"Brother…" Enrico grasps my shoulder, face grim.

I swallow hard and push myself upright, swaying. "The basement…"

We descend into musky darkness. Groans and whimpers echo from behind metal doors lining the dank stone corridor. My gut twists with fury and revulsion. But she's here. I can feel it.

At the end of the hall, we stop before an ancient oak door barred with rusted iron. As Enrico and I pry back the warped planks, the stench hits me like a blow—blood, sweat, fear.

My knees nearly buckle. Chained to the grimy floor, hair matted and clothes torn, is my Anya. Her deadened gaze lifts to meet mine, reignited with life as moonlight floods her cell.

"V-Vlad?" Her voice quivers with disbelief as she utters my name, as though beholding a dream.

I crush her fiercely to my chest, a broken whisper against her hair. "I'm here, my love... I'm here..."

Her tears flow freely now as she clings to me, desperately.

Quickly, I remove my thick fur coat and wrap Anya's frail frame in its warmth, trying to shield her from this dank cell's chill. She trembles like a frightened deer in my arms. I tighten my embrace, stroking her matted hair as her tears soak my shirt.

"Shhh. You're safe now... I have you," I murmur. With utmost care, I lift Anya's diminished weight and settle us both atop the moldy straw pallet. She immediately curls into me, head tucked beneath my chin. My throat tightens at how she seeks comfort and safety in my presence, even after enduring gods know what torments here.

"Rest easy, my heart," I rasp, continuing to stroke her hair as her breathing evens out. "I'll get you home."

*B*lood pounds in my ears as we cut our way through the labyrinthine halls of Roan's lair. The battle fever still simmers in my veins, but finding Anya has pacified the savage beast within. My only thoughts now are of getting her to safety.

I cradle Anya close, shielding her with my body as we push through clashing warriors in the grand foyer. My forces have subdued the remnants of Roan's wolves. As their new Alpha by conquest, they kneel in surrender, pledging allegiance to my pack. But there will be time for consolidation later—right now, I need to get Anya away from this place.

Enrico and Thane gather our warriors, their faces stone masks splattered with gore. We have won the day, but the bitter price paid in blood darkens the mood of victory. I nod to Enrico. "See that Roan is secured as our prisoner until I decide his fate. Guard him well."

Hoisting the massive oak doors open, I step out into the crisp night air, breathing deeply to dispel the choking stench of battle. Anya shivers in my arms, frail and bird-like. I pull my fur cloak tighter around her bare shoulders and pick up the pace, heading for the tree line.

The forest embraces us in moon-dappled shadows. Anya relaxes slightly as we put distance between ourselves and that monstrous place. But she stays silent, face buried against my chest as if she fears this is only a dream.

My feet pound against the ground, devouring the miles beneath them. My sole purpose is to protect Anya, shield her from harm, and bring her to safety. Her heartbeat, delicate and fragile, beats alongside mine like a captive bird longing for freedom. Nothing else matters but getting her home, tending to her injuries, and helping her broken spirit regain the strength and will to soar free once more.

We journey on. Anya drifts in and out of consciousness, drained and exhausted. When the dense woods finally thin ahead, emotion closes my throat. Our cabin, nestled in the valley just as I left it. *Home.*

My pace slows on the overgrown path. "We're here, my love," I rasp, my voice ragged. Anya peers up, eyes drinking in the cozy stone and timber structure. Her lips form a ghost of a smile—the first I've seen since rescuing her.

A snapping branch whips my head around, senses flaring. I ease Anya aside, settling her gently on the front porch's steps. She murmurs in confusion, not yet fully awake.

"Shh..." I soothe. "Rest here for a little while, my heart." I ease her head down and rise slowly, every muscle coiled tight. My eyes scan the dark tree line intently, searching for the source of the noise. An owl calls mournfully in the distance. Otherwise, only the whisper of wind stirs the leaves, carrying no trace of unnatural sounds or scents.

Gradually, I begin to relax. Likely just a small creature foraging in the underbrush, setting my battle-honed instincts on high alert over nothing. I turn back to Anya, ready to gather her into my arms again.

That's when I see it—the flecks of coarse fur snagged on the brambles, trails of massive pawprints in the muddy earth... *Wolf shifters.* But no members of my pack—currently laying siege under Enrico in Roan's territory. These are hostile strangers crossing into my lands uninvited and with violent intent.

My lips peel back from lengthening teeth. A vicious snarl reverberates through my barrel chest as fur ripples to take the place of skin. No one threatens what is mine and lives.

As if in response to the murderous rage now pounding through me, Boris steps out of the shadows. I will rip his traitorous heart out with my teeth for threatening Anya. Soon, four hulking fighters fan out beside him.

"You should have stayed gone, boy." Boris spits in the dirt, beady eyes deranged. "I'll take pleasure in ending you properly this time... right after I've had my fun with your worthless bitch."

A ferocious roar tears from my chest. The insult against my mate propels me forward, a blur of claws and fury. I bring down the first brute easily, tearing open his throat in a spray of hot blood. Whirling, I snap another's spine with vicious efficiency.

But the others surround me swiftly, raining blows and splitting my skin with their talons. I thrash violently, dragging down another even as gnashing teeth gouge my shoulder. Sheer desperation fuels me. I will die before letting them touch Anya.

Through the snarling tangle of limbs, I glimpse Boris' hulking form stalking towards where Anya lies vulnerable and unconscious, dagger glinting red in the fading light.

"NOOOOO!" I scream hoarsely, throwing my attackers off. But their grips only tighten, muscles bulging as I strain futilely. Triumph lights Boris' pig-eyes. He raises the blade, aiming for Anya's heart.

A deafening roar shatters the night. Boris whirls just as a giant fur-covered dark mass collides with him —eight feet and five hundred pounds of furious grizzly. The dagger goes flying as Boris hits the ground hard. He scarcely has time to shriek before mighty jaws close over his skull with a sickening crunch.

My opponents stumble back, bellowing in terror as more beasts burst from the trees—Ursa clan warriors in bear form, savage and unstoppable. In seconds, they make short work of Boris' outmatched followers.

Now shifted into my human form, I drop to my knees, gasping harshly as the last body hits the ground. "Anya!" *Thank the ancestors...* I crawl desperately towards where she lies motionless in the trampled grass.

Before I reach her, a figure leaps between us, crouching protectively over Anya's prone form.

"Stand down!" comes the thundering order nearby.

My vision is blurring, but I make out the glint of pale blonde hair and piercing sapphire eyes. *Sasha*, captain of the Ursa Elite guard.

Staggered footsteps approach from behind. I try twisting around only for agony to seize my battered body. A heavy hand settles on my shoulder. Turning my head takes monumental effort. I squint up at the battle-scarred face looming above me like something from a fever dream. Dark hair, granite jaw, chestnut eyes I know better than my own.

"Hello, brother..." Gavriil rumbles.

My throat works, but only coughs out red flecks. "You... came..." I choke out.

Gavriil kneels beside me with surprising gentleness. "Did you truly think I would abandon you?" His eyes tighten at my injuries. "Rest now. The nightmare is over."

The last of my strength finally flees, darkness clouding my vision. But I force out ragged words past blood-soaked lips, clinging desperately to consciousness:

"Anya... protect her... please..."

Gavriil clasps my shoulder. "She's safe, brother," he assures me. "We shall watch over your mate as one of our own. But you've pushed yourself to the brink. It's time to heal and recover." He wavers as he grips me tighter. "*Do not* leave me alone in this world... Vlad..." His expression hardens, fierce maroon eyes glistening with held-back emotion. "I've already lost my most beloved mate. I couldn't bear losing you, too."

His voice fades away, along with the pain.

The roar of my pulse slows to a tranquil lull. Anya is protected, with Sasha watching over her. Gavriil is by my side. My wounds will mend. For now, blessed darkness beckons, promising much-needed rest...

I surrender to it fully, allowing it to claim me.

28

VLAD

Sunlight streaming through gauzy curtains stirs me awake. I blink against the unaccustomed brightness. Crisp linen sheets rustle as I shift upright, taking in the luxurious bedroom.

Velvet drapes hang heavily over the wide windows, offering a view of the meticulously maintained gardens. Rainbow prisms dance across the walls, cast by crystal chandeliers that hang from the high ceiling. The massive four-poster bed could easily accommodate four people, its intricately carved posts spiraling up to support the embroidered canopy above. A pitcher of water and glass sit atop the nightstand, accompanied by neatly stacked white towels.

Polished black leather shoes stand beside a

mahogany dresser, a sleek bespoke suit hanging ready to be worn.

I rise slowly, muscles stiff and sore. But my wounds seem well on their way towards mending, the pain muted to a background ache. I make my way to the window and push back the drapes.

Warm spring air spills over my face. I breathe in deep, sorting through the scents of blooming vines and fresh earth. Beneath it all, a familiar note—cedar and aged timber, worn leather, and crackling hearth fires. The lingering fragrance of my childhood home, my father's estate in Saint Petersburg. And now, Gavriil's seat of power. I haven't set foot on these sprawling grounds in almost a decade. However long I've been here recovering, my brother has clearly been a gracious host.

A loud trill grabs my attention. In the garden below, Samara strolls along a cobblestone path, arm in arm with an auburn-haired young woman. It's Mila—sister to one of my brother's Elite guards, Dima. They stop to admire the budding yellow tulips swaying gently in the breeze.

I turn reluctantly from the vibrant view, my thoughts drifting back to Anya as I dress in the fine clothes laid out for me. My fingers fumble with the white gold and diamond cufflinks, a burning desire to have her by my side once again pulsing through every fiber of my being. But Gavriil's words echo in my mind—she is safe. Despite my overwhelming need to personally shield her from all danger, I must trust in that, and in the loyalty of the Elite Ursa warriors Gavriil dispatched to guard her.

Fully dressed, I make my way silently into the hall, zoning in unerringly on Gavriil's location. Pale light filters in through the arched windows lining the corridor. A ghostly gleam falls on our ancestors' stern faces as they peer down from their oil paintings hung in gilded frames. The study's polished walnut doors hang slightly ajar, a familiar silhouette visible through the gap. I push them open and step inside.

"Brother. It's good to see you awake," Gavriil says, waving me into his lavish office. He wraps up a call, then sets down the phone, his expression inscrutable. He's dressed immaculately as always, in a black bespoke suit and turtleneck, wearing it like ill-fitting armor. The outfit's darkness only enhances the new creases and scars etched into his face and the hollowness in his eyes. Cruel devastation consumes him, a sight I have never witnessed before. Without question, the loss of Luciana has ripped Gavriil's very soul apart.

I approach the broad desk, taking in the organized stacks of papers and maps. "How long was I out?" I grumble.

"Nearly a week. That last clash was... grueling." His tone makes it clear I needn't recount the bloody specifics. "Enrico's forces continue monitoring the situation, but the enemy is largely subdued now."

I absorb this quietly. My reckless push to reclaim Anya brought us to the brink. If not for Gavriil's reinforcements... I suppress a shudder at how close I came to losing everything.

A question surfaces through the fog of my memories. "What of Roan? Is he imprisoned for his crimes?"

Gavriil's expression shutters as he rises from the seat. He turns away under the pretense of stoking the hearth fire. "Unfortunately, after we brought him here, he attempted to escape." His knuckles go white on the iron poker. "He injured several of my men before we could restrain him again."

When he faces me once more, his eyes are hard as flint. "There was no choice after that. Roan had proven too dangerous to keep alive." His mouth thins. "We had to put an end to it."

I nod slowly, reading the truth between his terse words. Roan is dead by my brother's command. One less demon to haunt this world.

"You did what was necessary," I say firmly. "Some threats cannot be contained."

Gavriil's rigid shoulders relax slightly at the indulgence in my tone. His piercing stare meets mine with a sense of relief.

"Listen, Gavriil…" I stammer, my voice trembling with emotion. "I am forever in your debt. Had you not arrived with your Elite team—"

He cuts me off with a raised hand, mouth tightening. "You would have done the same for me." His shoulders curve inward slightly before he recovers. "Hell… you *already* did."

"Brother," I hurry to say, reaching his desk in two long strides. "The gods know I had my reservations about your union with Luciana. But I would never— *ever*—forsake your mate." The weight of my words hangs heavy in the air, stirring up painful memories and overwhelming guilt within me. "I failed…" My voice drops to a whisper. "I have failed you and our clan."

I grip the desk's smooth slab of maple wood to steady myself.

Gavriil's intense gaze pierces through me, his silence stretching on for what feels like an eternity.

Finally, he speaks in a low growl, his voice heavy with sorrow. "I *know* what happened, Vlad."

I start. "What do you mean?" I ask, heart bolting into a gallop.

He turns towards the window, shoulders rigid. When he speaks again, his tone is clipped, controlled. "Right after the attack, when..." he trails off, unable to finish the sentence. His pain is too raw, too overwhelming to put into words. Gavriil swallows hard, then continues in a wry tone. "Grisha came after me next. I fought back with all my might, and as I did, I recognized the fresh damage on him." He pauses. "*Your scent* was fixed on every dire gash and mottled bruise on his filthy pelt." He gives me a small, lopsided smile before walking around the desk to stand in front of me.

"That is how I know," he continues, a glint of pride flickering in his darkened gaze. "You gave every ounce of your strength in that battle, Vlad." His hand lands on my shoulder and presses it firmly. When it slides to cup my cheek, I know the empath in him is reading me like an open book—and I hold nothing back. All my guilt, sorrow, and grief pour forth, as I understand the immense pain of losing one's fated mate. This tragedy will weigh on him for eternity. It's already reshaped him into a different man. Formidable, yet tormented.

His eyes glisten with forthcoming tears, but he

fights them back with fierce determination. "My brother," Gavriil's voice is low and soothing, "you fought valiantly."

I grip his arm, emotion choking my voice. "Gavriil..." *I'm sorry I could not save Luciana.* The words feel wholly inadequate for a grief so profound.

"I'm afraid I must leave you," he cuts me off, his walls rising once more. "I've been summoned to Paris for a meeting with the Deveraux witches. I'm taking Samara with me... You're welcome to stay for as long as you wish." He gives me a meaningful stare. "This will always be your home, *Volodya*." A brief smile curls the corner of his lips.

With that, he spins on his heels, heading towards the doorway.

"What became of Grisha?" I force out, lest the restless question consumes me.

"I gave him the end he deserved," he replies cryptically. With a casual flick of his hand, he tosses on a rich black fur coat. As the luxurious material settles over his shoulders, I catch the faintest musky scent rising from it—it's unmistakable.

I remain frozen as realization dawns. "Wait," I gasp in shock and disbelief. "Is that...?"

Gavriil throws me a malicious grin, his eyes shadowed with intense hatred.

I don't need to hear him say it. The fur coat draped across his broad shoulders—*it was fashioned from Grisha's pelt.* It's become my brother's trophy, a symbol of his ruthless power. But also, a cruel reminder of the sacrifice he's made and can never take back.

"Oh." He stops abruptly at the doorway, eyes glinting with a mischievous spark. "Do take a stroll in the courtyard," he suggests with a sly smirk. "I have a feeling you'll find it quite enchanting this morning."

29

VLAD

find Anya sitting alone on a wrought iron bench, beneath the snow-flecked pine trees edging the manor gardens. She's facing away, towards the sunrise creeping over the distant hills. Something about the set of her slender shoulders speaks of pensiveness, even melancholy. But as I crunch down the gravel pathway, her chin lifts, and she turns to me with a blossoming smile that could rival the dawn.

"You're awake," she breathes, rising to meet my open arms. I crush her close, letting her subtle floral scent infuse me with comfort, as my lips find the tender skin behind her ear.

"How do you feel?" Anya pulls back just far

enough to search my face with concern shadowing her dark eyes.

I smooth a thumb over her delicate brow until it eases. "Right as rain now that you're here, my love."

With a soft laugh, Anya tugs me down beside her on the cold iron seat. I keep her tucked close against my side, unwilling to lose the connection of touch I've craved since slipping into darkness after that last brutal battle.

"Gavriil told me not to worry, that you would come out of it soon enough," Anya says. "But when the hours stretched on and you didn't wake..." She shivers.

I wrap my arms more firmly around her. "Hush. It's alright. I'm back now, and I'm not going anywhere." I kiss the top of her head, breathing in the floral scent of her hair.

We sit quietly for a time, taking comfort from the solid warmth of each other, as the sun climbs higher to melt the frost cloaking the dormant garden. The peaceful setting belies the violence and bloodshed that brought us here. But the worst is behind us now.

Birdsong fills the crisp morning air, underscored by the cheerful burbling of a nearby fountain. Anya absently traces her fingers over the back of my hand, touch feather-light, as if reassuring herself this is real. I tighten my hold on her, vowing to keep her safe from further harm.

At length, Anya speaks again, a teasing lilt lifting the pensiveness that shrouded her. "I can't believe you never told me you belonged to one of the most powerful shifter families in all of Russia."

I rub the back of my neck sheepishly. "It never seemed relevant. I didn't exactly part on good terms with my clan."

Anya smoothes a hand over my chest, tenderness in her gaze. "Well, you have a beautiful family, Vlad. And a home here whenever you wish."

Her words sink into my heart. With Anya by my side, this place could feel like home again. I press a kiss to her temple, my arms curling her closer. "If you like it here, wait until you see my estate in Rome. Now *that* will take your breath away."

I'm rewarded with a grin that warms me like the climbing sun at my back. But all too soon, Anya's expression clouds again. She picks at a thread on her sleeve, not meeting my eyes.

"What is it?" I prod gently. "Talk to me, my love."

With a heavy sigh, Anya lifts her troubled gaze to mine. "I just can't help thinking... our worlds are so different, Vlad. Yours and mine. I'm not sure I'll ever fit into the life you were born to."

Her vulnerability pierces me. I take her hands, ducking to catch her lowered eyes. "You mustn't say that. You are everything to me, Anya. I'm more than happy to make room for you in my life."

But uncertainty lingers in the crease between her brows. She chews her lip, clearly wrestling with something. Finally, Anya asks haltingly, "And what about... What if it wasn't *only* me?" She pauses, taking a shaky breath. "What if there was a pup? Or two?"

Her vulnerable eyes search my face. "Would you make room for them as well?"

My breath catches, pulse skittering. "Anya... are you... are we...?" *A child... our child?* The thought leaves me staggered. I hold onto Anya rightly, meeting her uncertain gaze unwaveringly.

She nods, a fragile hope dawning through her anxiety. "I know it's much too soon, completely unexpected." Her hands twist together. "And I'll understand if you'd rather wait until..."

I cut her off, crushing Anya fiercely to my pounding heart. "Moon of my life! How can you think for one second I would wish this any other way?" I grasp her shoulders so I can see the wonder blooming in her eyes. "Learning we created new life together... I've never felt such joy."

Emotion chokes me, spilling from my eyes. I kiss each of Anya's flushed, damp cheeks. "Our child..." My broad palm covers her still-flat belly. "I cannot wait to meet them."

Tears slip down Anya's pinkish cheeks even as she beams. "Truly?"

"Truly, my love." I pepper her face with tender kisses until she laughs. "I cannot wait to welcome our children into the world. However many we are blessed with." I kneel before her, hands framing her belly in reverence.

"They will want for nothing. Our sons and daughters will be showered with more love than they know what to do with." I look up at Anya, heart over-flowing. "Thank you for this gift, my mate."

Anya pulls me up into a fierce kiss full of promise. I lift her easily into my arms, relishing her lilting laughter as it echoes off the stately manor walls. Our future unfurls before us, bright and beautiful. The coming springtime will see our family grow.

I nuzzle against Anya's throat, memorizing her beloved scent laced now with the new sweetness of motherhood. My entire world cradled safe in my arms. I silently vow to be the father our children deserve, to shield them from darkness and guide them into the moonlight.

I carry Anya over the threshold into the sunlit warmth of the house. No matter what storms may rage outside these walls, we have all we need within. As long as I have Anya by my side, and soon our precious children, I am home.

ABOUT THE AUTHOR

Silvana G. Sánchez is the USA TODAY bestselling author of sinfully addictive dark fantasy new adult novels *Ash and Snow, Steel and Stone, Written in Blood,* and more paranormal and fantasy romance stories, including the *Vesely Academy* series. She lives in Mexico with her husband, son, and two adorable Shih-Tzus she calls her dragons. When not plotting away in her writing den, she's known to poke eyes in her practice as an ophthalmologist.

For more information:
silvanagsanchez.com
sgs.author@gmail.com